The Side Chick

The Side Chick

Katt

www.urbanbooks.net

Urban Books, LLC
300 Farmingdale Road, NY-Route 109
Farmingdale, NY 11735

ISBN 13: 978-1-62286-482-9
ISBN 10: 1-62286-482-4

First Trade Paperback Printing May 2017
Printed in the United States of America

10 9 8 7 6 5 4 3 2 1

This is a work of fiction. Any references or similarities to actual events, real people, living or dead, or to real locales are intended to give the novel a sense of reality. Any similarity in other names, characters, places, and incidents is entirely coincidental.

Distributed by Kensington Publishing Corp.
Submit Orders to:
Customer Service
400 Hahn Road
Westminster, MD 21157-4627
Phone: 1-800-733-3000
Fax: 1-800-659-2436

Chapter One

Mary Bivens

"Hey, Ma." Melissa came down the aisle, greeting me. She was her usual sarcastic self. She then bent down to give me a hug. "Where's Dad? Back there helping Clifton straighten his tie or something like that?" She left a seat between us as she sat down giving me the side-eye.

"Nope, he's not back there helping your brother. I'm not sure if he's coming, actually. That would be too much like right if you ask me. So you can just slide over and leave that seat for a parent who really cares."

"Aw, Ma, come on now. Don't be like that. Dad cares real deep down inside. He's just going through a midlife crisis or whatever it is you old people call it once you go over the hill in age." Melissa tried taking up for her father who had dropped the ball on his fatherly duties more than once lately.

Even with her physically looking just like me and having attributes of my attitude added to her personality, Melissa could sometimes be just as nonchalant and coldhearted as Charles if not worse than him. Money is not the root of all evil; genes are, in this case. And my daughter was definitely starting to morph into my once better half.

"Melissa, please busy yourself with the applications and silly little games on your cell phone as you usually do and stay out of grown folks' business. Thanks," I snapped, not in the mood for her "I'm grown, now I can talk how I want to" ass running off at the mouth. She, as always, was trying my patience. I was deep off into my own world. I was too occupied cursing out her insensitive father via text message, which was the only way we could communicate as of late without calling each other damn near everything except for the child of God.

"Okay, dang, Ma, just take a chill pill. I'm falling back like you asked. Ain't no need to get all crazy with it. But just let me know if you need me to come up out of a child's place to pin my little brother alongside you." She continued being a smart ass, then shifted in her seat so her back would be to me.

How rude and ballsy of her. Had we not been in a roomful of judgmental people, I would have collared her ass up like I had so many times before in the past. I didn't know how many times I'd warned her about that flip mouth, but whatever. I hated having to remind her that attending a four-year university didn't make her grown; well, not when it came to speaking to your elders.

"Your place is going to be six feet deep down in a grave if you speak slick one more time, Melissa," I warned. I leaned over and delivered my threat coldly, then sat straight up in my seat. Between Melissa and her father, I was gonna end up dry popping an anxiety pill. She was tap dancing on nerves he'd already burnt out.

While all the other senior parents were socializing with one another, my fingers were floating across the touch screen keypad of my phone, texting my husband a gang of messages. I hoped when he read each one his eyes would burn and fear the hot, fiery rage I felt.

Our life and what I always dreamed it would be was in a complete shambles. I was angry, hurt, and fed up with him ignoring not only me but our family as well. He had become beyond distant and an asshole. I was used to him not showing up at home for dinner; that had become almost second nature to him. And I was immune to Charles even emotionally checking out on our marriage when he did come home. I would just read a book or do what I did, no biggie. However, no matter how much I tried, I hadn't gotten used to the sting of being out in public alone. That part was still killing me as all of our mutual friends would be arm in arm at various events asking me the million dollar question: "Where's Charles?" Most times I'd make up some sort of mild conceivable answer. Yet, the last few times I was finding myself having cotton mouth and running out of lies to tell. Some of my close friends could tell something was wrong, but I played it off the best I could.

I had a reputation to uphold, and it was more important for me to stand beside my husband in front of the crowded room than it was to flash my flossy wedding ring in place of him. We were a team. Well, we were supposed to be a team. That's how things always were from Jump Street and should be now. Truth be told, I'd trade each one of these perfectly cut flawless karats on my finger for a cereal box plastic gem in a heartbeat if Charles's love for me would come with it. The selfish human who now wasn't here for his family was not the man I met, fell in love with, or married. I'd been driving myself crazy with the puzzling question of "Why is this happening?" In my eyes I did everything I could to make a great household for him and our kids; but I guessed I dropped the ball somehow, let him tell it.

We lived in a very exclusive, upper-class area of town my husband worked hard to make happen. Any person from any ethnicity was welcome on our block. As long as their pay grade or social status could fit the bill they were good. I was sure the color of a person's skin was discussed and ridiculed behind closed doors, but within our community the only color that mattered was money, that almighty dollar. Class could be purchased, friends could be bribed, and reputations meant everything. I lived here solely because of Charles. Matter of fact, as sad and pathetic as it may sound, I'd spent half of my entire life being everything I was for Charles. He was, simply put, my ultimate everything. In our world, the sun rose and set because of him. Now that he had chosen to "do him," as the young people say, I was sitting here alone in this auditorium looking like an angry, lost puppy dog.

"Parents, please stand and applaud the next graduating class of the Prestigious Collegiate Preparatory Academy. I present to you our seniors." The principal proudly started the pinning ceremony, introducing and bringing out my son and his peers.

I couldn't believe my baby boy was about to be a graduate and a grown man within a few months. I didn't know where time had gone. Nevertheless, I was proud of him and all of his friends, being that I had chaperoned the majority of them at sleepovers, parties, and afterschool play dates since their kindergarten ages. Part of the PCPA promise was familiarity and consistency among its population. They prided themselves on keeping a close-knit and exclusive environment. And for the elitism, their tuition was a hefty price.

The Prestigious Collegiate Preparatory Academy had gotten deep into Charles's checking account for educating both of our children. Melissa joined the PCPA family in the fourth grade, after being on the waitlist for three years. They didn't have a flexible admission process, but the wait was more than worth it. My daughter's diploma opened up several doors for her that would have otherwise been slammed in her face. Plainly put, her diploma was an expensive piece of paper that said she came from somewhere. God willing, Clifton's would be the same to him; at least, that's what we were banking on.

Tucking my phone away, it wasn't a hard stretch to stop wanting to reach through my cell's screen and spit in his absent father's face and redirect my attentions on my son. I stood and clapped for Clifton as one of the loudest parents in the room. My hands started to slightly sting as I slammed them together twice as hard since Charles was not there to hold us down.

My baby boy had worked hard. He was expected to graduate with honors and deserved respect for that. The bullshit drama going on between his dad and me wasn't going to make me rain on his parade; not now, not ever. I hated when bickering mothers and fathers couldn't grow up enough to coparent. For all of Clifton's hard work, accomplishments, and constant dedication to staying on track while facing and beating temptation, he deserved a proud and present parent to be in the audience. It was only right for me to shake his hand, hug him, and congratulate him on a job well done thus far. I was going to be that parent and do just that. Support and encouragement can push kids far, and I wanted mine, or should I say ours, to be the best.

While the principal was delivering his positive, uplifting message, I dug my phone back out. Overjoyed in the moment, I started snapping pictures. But that warm, fuzzy emotion was soon short-lived. Before I knew it, my vindictive side had once again reared its ugly head. With malice boiling in my heart, I started sending them to Charles with petty, snide captions typed underneath each.

Our son Clifton was handsome, debonair, and looked like fresh, crispy money at all times. We kept him on point. He was the spitting image of his dad who, by the way, still looked great for his age. Charles, the main provider, made it possible for him to have a Rolex on his wrist, Ray-Bans on his face, a Hermès belt on his waist, and Prada shoes on his feet. If nothing else, I could never take away the fact that Charles has done financially right by his children. Never ever has either of them eaten from a struggle spoon or missed a hearty meal because of money being short. Charles actually has a bad habit of throwing money at the kids to make things right when he messes up. Although I despised the way my husband had been treating me, the kids seemed to be ignoring his obvious transgressions against the family unit as long as the money and gifts kept flowing. Those two, unlike me, had not made their father their entire world.

As Clifton looked around the room and caught eye contact with me, he smiled and winked, making me smile and wink back. He was not a momma's boy by far, but he knew how to charm the ladies. I could tell from how much he kept his iPhone up to his ear; he could run game. That was something he picked up from his now-sneaky dad, running game. But that was all right. It was all good. God don't like ugly from me or anyone else. Karma was one bad, mean, evil bitch when she needed to be. In my feelings, I wanted Charles to feel some type of way as well. If I was hurting, he needed to hurt and feel the burn as well.

Back in the day, I had my own way of always getting what I wanted. I didn't want to be judged and hoped I wouldn't be. I used to play mind games with Charles, using the kids as pawns. Whereas some women won't let the dads see their kids, I overwhelmed Charles with pictures of our two. If Melissa cried scraping her knee, I sent a picture of her tears because I knew he'd die to protect his precious baby girl. If Clifton picked up a toy basketball, I sent the picture along with a message saying, This boy needs his dad. And at least once a day, I made them call their dad and leave him voice-mails so he could hear their baby babbles and tiny voices. There was no shame in my game about playing mind manipulation games with Charles to bring and keep him home. I took a vow to God to fight for my family. And that was exactly what I was going to keep doing even after all of these years. *If he thinks it's going to be over that easy just because the kids we made together are of age and doing their own thing, he's sadly mistaken.*

The audience clapping once more was what brought me out of my deep-seated thoughts. They were announcing who the newly elected senior class officers were, which didn't matter to me since Clifton hadn't run. Yet, I knew the actual pinning ceremony was next. They had not changed the flow of the ceremony during the three years since I'd been in this same auditorium for Melissa, so I was more than familiar with what came next. By homeroom, each student was announced and then pinned by the parents while a photographer captured the moment. As a lumped formed in my throat, knowing all the "Where is Charles?" questions were forthcoming, I polished my five-karat wedding ring with hot breath, drying it with my eyeglass cloth so at least I portrayed a happily married wife for the camera. If I was going to be on display for all of our friends to see, no doubt about it, I was going to shine bright. I would keep my fronts up. To hell with all of that pitiful "lamb going to the slaughter" garbage mentality most bitter and broken women displayed.

Charles Bivens

The room was dark. Except for the flickers coming from the stream of candles that where strategically lined up it was hard for me to focus. Truth be told now was not the time or place I wanted to concentrate on anything other than relaxing. There was a soft R&B song playing. It was one of my favorites I always asked for, but I could barely hear the melody because of how hard the bass was beating into the small room. And within the room, there was me, a female, and a muscular male security guard who was standing by the door with his back turned but his ears open. Of course, he was there to make sure I didn't take the girl's cookie without paying for it. I knew he was getting paid, and this was his job to do, but if I were him, I'd be feeling like no more than a creep or sexual predator. But hey, I guess like they say, to each his own. Sometimes the end justifies the means.

The main attraction, or the reason I was there, had just whispered in my ear causing my manhood to jump as she went to work. Her stage name was China White. "Why?" some may ask. Because her mere touch made you feel like you were on drugs. It may have seemed like it was just a rumor or a myth, but to me it was reality. I could bear witness to her power. I'd been addicted to her back room loving for the last few months. Ever since this gritty, infamous strip spot opened back up, I'd been damn near a regular.

The Gentleman's Spot had been operating for years off and on whenever they could avoid the cops raiding the place. The women here were built like brick houses. Beautiful and willing to get bodied in the beds they had in the back rooms. This place was a horny man's American dream. Everyone who is anyone came here for a retreat from the real world: politicians, engineers, teachers, doctors, successful entrepreneurs, and even lawyers.

Today I brought one of my associates I dealt with from time to time. Although Jake and I came from much different backgrounds we shared the common bond most men—well, the straight ones—share: the love of pussy.

After a long meeting and a few shots from the expensive bottle of bourbon I kept in my locked desk drawer, he revealed he was having problems with his wife. Easily feeling his pain of being linked up with a woman for years who was more into being a soccer mom than being a freak in the bed, I knew what he needed to take the edge off.

When we first pulled up he was more than hesitant to get out the car, but with the promise of sheer satisfaction on the other side of the wall, Jake caved in to the notion of cheating on his wife. I promised him that although the club was located in what some would say was a seedy part of town, he was good; we were good.

The club's well-to-do clientele were what kept them afloat. Whenever the city raided clubs that were operating without permits and such, the owners were tipped off early, and the doors were shut until the cases were closed. This spot had been closed down for months at a time behind the city trying to crack down. Today, luckily for all of us sexual savages, the spot was open for business and I was enjoying the perks.

"Charlie, baby. I think your phone is ringing." China White lifted her head from my lap, telling me something I already knew. "You want me to stop so you can answer it or what? I mean, I'm in the zone, but—"

"Yeah, I know it's ringing, but hell naw, don't worry about that. Just concern yourself with keeping that dick wet with your spit. That's all daddy care about right now is your neck game." Tapping the top of her head for her to drop it back down, I then dropped my own head back so I could finish getting serviced.

Her mouth was legendary, warm and wet just like a vagina. I'd paid her a hundred bucks for me and a hundred for Jake for twenty-five minutes of her time, and I'd wanted all twenty-five of them spent with her full and pouty lips wrapped snugly around my manhood and making sure my homeboy was happy. I wasn't concerned about digging my phone from my pocket and answering it. Not only was the continuous vibration from it feeling too damn good along with the head job, but I knew who the constant caller was and why they were trying to reach me.

My son's senior pinning ceremony was today, and my overly dramatic wife wanted to know why I wasn't there. I knew by right I should have been there by her side to support our son, but what could I say? I guessed it was just another one of them times I dropped the ball I'd been accused by her and the kids of being so guilty of doing. I was living life on my own terms now and not for anyone else.

I wanted to just pick up, be real, and tell her the truth. I wanted to just be black-hearted and let her know I was preoccupied with the dick she used to worship for years stuffed down the next bitch's throat. If only it were that easy. Knowing Mary the way I did, she was cursing me out via text as well as sending me guilt pictures of Clifton up on stage. That was her thing.

I'd picked up on her game a long time ago but allowed her to think she was slick. She wanted the pictures of him to tug at my heart enough to pull me back to her, but that trick wasn't going to work now that the kids were grown. Part of the reason I fell out of love with Mary was because she was too predictable. I was at the point in my life where excitement was a must, and consistency was something I ran from. Mary claimed she knew what my problem was. She kept insisting that I was having a midlife crisis. And although some part of that accusation may have been true, so damn what? I lost myself, and I buried my true desires of living life on the edge for years.

Now was my time to do what daddy wanted, and if letting White China suck me off until I came twice in the middle of the afternoon was what made me happy then so be it.

My daughter, Melissa, had already left home and was in college. She was staying on campus and to be honest I couldn't have been happier. Even though she was a daddy's girl and served as a buffer against most of her mother's unwarranted verbal attacks, she still worked my last nerve being a spoiled brat. I had no one to blame when it came to that. I created that monster; now I had to deal with it.

My son, Clifton, was a senior in high school and was most definitely going to leave the nest once he graduated. I was counting down the days just as he was. The boy was barely abiding by the curfew his mother had in place now and it was driving her crazy. He was in a rush to be a grown man, hungry for his freedom away from Mary. And, truth be told, I didn't blame him one bit. She was overbearing and worked the nerves of everyone in the entire household. My wife thought he was a spitting image of me and he just might have been.

I was desperate for my freedom and would get it once he walked across that stage. I swore on everything I loved and this good head White China was giving me that I was going to serve Mary divorce papers on the day Clifton received his high school diploma. With both of our offspring not being kids anymore, I didn't have to fake it 'til we made it any longer.

I'd been over my marriage for some time now. Despite Mary asking me time and time again what happened to the dedicated love we once shared, I could not answer her. As much as she begged, I had no clear reply. One day, just like that, I fell out of love with her and our marriage. The next thing I knew, I had started falling in between the legs of a bunch of random women. I'd lost count of the legit number of women I'd had affairs with or just had sex when the notion hit me.

When I sat back and thought about it, I knew what my issue was. I was addicted to being in control, having women submit to me in ways my wife would not. I liked living out nasty fantasies, like this impromptu threesome, and doing whatever I wanted to women. That was how I had managed to sleep with so many different ones. I had a lot of needs that stayed needing to be fulfilled. Mary just didn't do it for me anymore. There was no excitement or flair in our bedroom like there was here with China White, my paid-for freak. And, outside of the bedroom, there was a ton of responsibility and a ton of nagging. The thought of it was making my stomach turn.

Right on time, probably because my dick was starting to go soft at the thought of Mary, ol' girl turned it up a few notches and got wild with it. She wasn't gonna let the session end without me being fully satisfied and shooting off a load with my newcomer friend doing the same. She wanted to make sure I would be eager to return and spend my money with her and no one else. I could tell from the way she made her tongue slip and slide down my shaft. She started hungrily kissing, licking, and spitting on my cock while tickling and grabbing on my balls. I had to slip off my loafers for how hard my toes kept curling up to her tantalizing tricks. My eyes kept rolling in the back of my head, and I was slowly losing my mind. She was sucking every ounce of control out of me, without once coming up for air, handling my piece like an instrument.

"You like all this dick me and him filling you up with?"

Before White China could answer, "Yes, daddy," she was taking all seven inches of Charles down her throat with complete ease. When she first got at the club, she was somewhat of an amateur in the sex department.

Scared to touch the dick, let alone be aggressive, now gifted, White China went in. Slurping, licking, sucking, head bobbing from the left to the right and the right to the left, she had now regular customers in a daze, almost speaking in tongues. Not being able to sit still, Charles raised his lower body off the oversized chair to meet each deep gulp White China now happily took.

Easily gaining the attention of his homeboy with her skills, Jake stood, dropping his own pants. With the security guard looking on, secretly pissed at the way the dancer he had a crush on seemed to be enjoying sucking Charles off, Jake eased the G-string down and off a thick-boned White China. Watching her wide ass bounce up and down and jiggle while she swallowed his homeboy's dick, Jake got down on his knees behind her. With one hand balanced on her protruding dunk, he used the other to guide his stiff meat down White China's crack. All into it, White China reached her hand backward and started to finger her own wet, hairy snatch.

Jake's dick grew harder as the veins started to bulge. Sensing what he wanted from past experiences, White China used both hands to reach back and spread her cheeks wide open. Not being able to stand it any longer, Jake gladly accepted the invitation, shoving his throbbing helmet-shaped dickhead into her asshole. With as much force as he could, he tried to ram through to the other side. White China didn't care, still holding her cheeks open so the Caucasian stallion could keep handling his business. Every time his homeboy went in harder, pounding from the rear, it made her take even more of Charles's seven inches without so much as gagging.

Charles didn't miss White China using her hands to stroke him, because she was throat fucking him royally.

Every few seconds, in his Southern-roots voice, he would yell out she was the best he ever had. And Jake, who never really wanted to get with her in the first place, but did at Charles's urging, was also screaming out White China's praises. The two white-collar men talking shit seemed to fuel her to get even more buck wild with it, throwing her ass up higher in the air for Jake's pleasure while burying her head deeper on Charles's dick.

With all three of them apparently in their own freaky world, rhythmically banging to the beat of the jazz music now playing louder, the security guard got heated, feeling left out of the loop and questioning why he even liked White China's freak ass in the first place. He knew that this was her job, but she was a little more off into these two customers than others. With folded arms, he leaned back against the wall pretending she was just another one of the wild, loose pussy tricks in the club. Knowing he needed this gig to pay the bills, he tried his best to mask his contempt for Jake, Charles, and especially White China. None of the three freaks in search of a nut cared one bit about his or their wives' feelings. It was what it was and would be what it would be.

Taking full advantage of her skills, I slid back and pushed myself as far as I could down her throat. The tip of my mushroom was tickling White China's tonsils, which was making my knees start to buckle. She was sucking for gold and about to strike it rich. Her tongue swirling up then around on my penis felt so damn good. There wasn't a stroke shorty didn't take or a drop she didn't swallow. I momentarily glanced upward to see the same crazy look on Jake's face that I had plastered on mine. He had busted as well. Mission accomplished. If only Mary knew how to please me like all the other women I cheated on her with I might still be at home happy or, better yet, sitting at that ceremony by her side.

"Are you good, Charlie? Or do you need another round to get you right?" she asked, coming up off her knees while wiping her mouth off and turning to see if Jake was smiling as well.

"Unfortunately, sexy, I have another engagement I must rush off to. But I'll be seeing you later this week for sure. You gonna be ready for me, right?"

"Of course. Well, I guess I will see you then. It's been fun, but I've gotta get back to the money, honey. Them dollars is calling my name and a bitch got bills to pay. Unless your boy here wanna go another round or two with this good cat I got purring in between my legs." Tossing me a hand towel and some foam antibacterial soap to clean myself up with, Jake declined, pulling his pants back up. She then collected the big tip we both blessed her with, as I always did, and disappeared from the dimly lit room.

And I've gotta get back to playing a role, I said to myself as I stood to get dressed. I wasn't going to make the actual pinning ceremony, but I was going to be just in time to make up for it. Within ten minutes, I had my tie back on and was walking out of the Gentleman's Spot to drop Jake back off at his car then be on my way to Clifton's high school.

Mary Bivens

Despite me thinking I'd be too weak or would break down in front of the audience, I stood like a proud mother beside Clifton after I pinned him a senior. The moment was not as bad as I thought it would be, but yet and still I was glad that it was over. Clifton was still in the back with his classmates and teacher; Melissa was chatting with a few girls she'd graduated with and were also there to support their younger siblings; and, as for me, I was in line with the other parents picking up the school's senior packet, which I knew was guaranteed to cost a gang of Charles's hard-earned money. He might have been done paying tuition, but he had a few thousand more to spend before Clifton's actual graduation. They had a senior winter trip, a senior spring trip, dues, dances, not to mention the prom. If Charles did divorce me, there might not have been any money left within our shared account for me to have in a settlement. I knew I would never get access to his personal account. He was much too slick-minded for that to happen.

"Mary, hey, girl." I heard a voice that made the hairs on my neck stand up. It was that damn Linda Oliver. Her middle daughter, Elizabeth, was in the same class as Clifton. And her oldest daughter, Amanda, graduated a year before Melissa. If there was a definition of "ass ache" in the dictionary, her picture would have most definitely been by it.

"Linda, hello." I put on the fakest sweet-sounding voice I could muster up then spun around to face her.

Linda was extremely tall; matter of fact, she was taller than the average man. Caucasian with stringy hair, she wore a lot of makeup to appear flawless even though her skin was severely damaged from acne. Hell-bent on putting on airs, she actually had a professional makeup artist come make her beautiful on a daily basis. Her husband's salary allowed for her to blow money recklessly, so the ache to my ass took full advantage of doing just that.

"So, Mary, how was your and the kids' summer? Did you guys do anything interesting I should know about?"

"Oh, it was absolutely wonderful," I lied, not able to come up with any details so quickly, and not willing to expose my truth. I mean, what was I supposed to tell her? That I spent most of it alone in the corner of the couch reading torrid love novels because Charles was busy spending time with his plethora of whores? Or that Melissa had to take classes in the summer to keep her academic-earned scholarship since she'd failed the courses during the winter semester partying like there was no tomorrow in sight? Nope, I wasn't going to tell her that my life and marriage had absolutely no fireworks or flair, and was just a mundane routine that had made me miserable. Doing that would be like committing society suicide. So instead I stood my ground saying as little as possible. It was a good thing Linda, vain as ever, loved talking about herself because she took over the entire conversation.

"Oh, that sounds nice. The family and I vacationed in Miami, don't you know? Then we went on a cruise just because. And, Mary, just when I thought we were done and we could retire our luggage, we spent a week in the Bahamas. Jerald took the whole summer off from surgeries for some much-needed family time, so it was nothing but fun, fun, fun. You know how it is when you have a husband who is as much in demand in his field as mine is."

Part of the reason I couldn't stand Linda was because she bragged too damn much. I hadn't asked, yet she was running down the three-month break to me without so much as taking a short breath. A fake smile was plastered on my face as she spoke but, in my mind, I was saying, *Bitch, please shut up and continue to do so each and every time you are in my presence.*

I did what I always did when I saw her coming: suck it up and count the seconds until some other poor wife had the misfortune of walking up on us. "Wow, that sounds like a beautiful way to spend the summer. I know the girls loved it." I purposely did not ask her any questions, hoping she'd catch the hint, but she failed to as my eyes

searched the room for the exit signs just in case someone
would hopefully yell out, "Fire."

"I'd say yes overall. Amanda especially loved the cruise
and the time we spent in Miami because she got to party,
drink, and be carefree. She didn't utter one complaint.
You know how it was when we were her age. Now, my
Elizabeth, however, had fun until her age became an issue. She got homesick whenever it was nighttime and she
had to go back to the room. I felt bad for my baby, but I
wasn't going to miss any quality time with the husband,
and I couldn't make Amanda stay and babysit her. We
just let her order room service and promised to get her
a new car in the spring. Jerald and I have already talked
about letting her take a friend next year. I tell you, these
kids are something else."

"Oh, okay." My response was even shorter than the
last. I wasn't trying to be blatantly rude, but I was ready
for her to go back over to her husband or find another
sounding board victim. She didn't, though. Linda ended
up walking down the line with me one overly detailed
event of her life at a time. By the time we picked up our
kids' senior packets, the kids were coming from the back
almost ready to leave.

Clifton came straight over and hugged me as he usually did. "Hey, Ma. Where's Dad at? Did he make it?"
was the first question he had the nerve to ask me. The
fact that we were in front of Linda was the worst part
of it all. She was so caught up in her own perfect world,
she had failed to even take notice that my other half was
missing in action. Like back when he was a little boy
and said the wrong thing out in public, I wanted to pop
him in the lips. It took everything in my power not to
shoot him with eye daggers. Sadly before I got a chance
to answer him or divert the conversation, Linda jumped
in putting her surgically altered nose in the air.

"Oh, yeah, Mary. That was what I wanted to ask you when I walked over, but I got so caught up in telling you about our long, obscenely expensive vacation."

Before I got a chance to answer her, Jerald walked over to our small huddle. Thank God for small miracles. I sighed a breath of relief, thinking he was about to drag his irritating wife away.

"Clifton, you looked mighty fine up there on that stage, young man," he complimented my son then shook his hand.

"Thank you, sir," Clifton accepted the compliment with a smile on his face.

"No problem. Make sure you keep up the good work and finish strong."

"Of course, sir. My pops wouldn't have it any other way."

"I'm sure of that too." Jerald chuckled. "He's done a fine job raising you and your sister." Turning his attention from Clifton, Jerald then addressed me. "Speaking of my old buddy, where is Charles at anyway? I was looking forward to seeing him here so I could invite him over for a poker party I'm hosting for the guys next weekend, a little alpha man time."

This time around, I had my lie prepared. "Oh, come on now, Jerald. You know how you and Charles are when it comes to work. He was upset to have to miss this ceremony but couldn't rip himself away from the office. He texted me something about the whole system crashing or something like that. You know I can't keep up with all those high-tech terms he knows. That type of stuff is way over my head." I'd strategically played against Jerald having to work crazy hours at the hospital so he wouldn't dispute my story.

Jerald grabbed my hand up and kissed it. "Like I tell Linda all the time, we work to keep our wives beautiful and stress free."

"You better put my wife's hand down, old man." Charles's voice cut through the crowd but pierced my ears like nails going across a chalkboard.

"Dad." Clifton was overly excited. Whereas he should have been asking him where the hot-fire hell he'd been and why he was late. But he didn't. It was all like it was "Dad for president" as it always was. I was the villain, and good old Dad could do no wrong. *Damn my son for being so weak-minded and biased.*

"Ah, the man I was just asking about." Jerald dropped my hand to shake my husband's. "Timing is something else, I tell ya. Mary just finished telling Linda and me that you were caught up in the office fixing the system from some sort of a crazy shutdown."

"Oh, she did? Okay, then, Mary. Well, we'll go with that story for now." He put on an asshole sarcastic grin and winked his right eye.

Instantly, as if on cue, my stomach curled up into knots. If looks could kill, Charles would have dropped dead on the spot. I went from being in disbelief that he'd even shown up, to wanting to choke him out for his flip mouth. He was dead-ass wrong for putting me on blast like that. I promised one day he was gonna get what he was looking for, one damn day.

"Oh, here comes Lizzie." Linda picked up on the apparent awkwardness. She wanted to get away from our ever-growing dysfunctional family, no doubt wanting to go gossip about what my husband had said. "Come on, sweetheart. Let's meet up with her." Tugging at Jerald's arm, she snatched him away all while looking at me with pity in her eyes.

Though she'd saved me from another moment of embarrassment, I wasn't looking forward to running into her again. *Damn Charles and his selfish ass.* I didn't have to explain my truth to uppity ass earlier, yet it was almost inevitable that I was going to have to now.

Charles Bivens

"Pops, for real? Aww naw, this is me?" Clifton asked with a big grin on his face.

"Yup, son. All you have to do is walk that stage and graduate. And, with the flick of the wrist, I'll transfer the title over into your name." I was happy to present my son with his first vehicle.

I'd given Melissa her first car on her graduation day. Though I had the money to give them cars in the tenth grade like their peers, I didn't want them to have so much freedom early on in their high school careers. The reason I needed Mary home to raise the kids was to make sure they stayed on track and we as parents kept some control. Both of my children needed to be successful. I didn't get my first car until I got a job and was able to pay for it out of my own pocket. But that didn't mean I didn't want one while I was in high school to take girls out on dates. Females turned me down on a daily basis for dates. Seriously, I didn't even get to go to the prom because I didn't have a car or access to one. The chicks at my school weren't fond of dating a dude with a bus pass. But, hey, I didn't blame them. I didn't want a bus pass either. Both of my parents worked their asses off for us to have the bare necessities. I honestly didn't blame them for how we struggled. If anything, it made me a much stronger man. My woes made me work harder to get more than what we had. So rewarding my kids was more a privilege and a tribute to my success than a chore.

"Hell yeah. I mean, thank you, Dad." He was so excited that he was cursing and stuttering at the same time. I knew he would be geeked. If I had been in his shoes, I guess I'd have been behaving the same way.

"No thanks needed, son. Just make sure you keep those grades up, walk that stage on time, and manage not to become a statistic by getting some girl pregnant." I laid the terms on the line. Now it was up to him to do the right thing.

He chuckled a little bit, probably at the last line, and then responded, "We have a deal. I won't let neither you or Mom down. I'm gonna stay on top of all my school-work. I swear to God."

I hadn't given Mary a second glance since earlier when I insensitively aired her out. I knew good and well I was dead wrong for doing so. The tension between us was super thick and our daughter, my self-appointed buffer, had disappeared somewhere with her friends. Mary didn't even know I was coming, let alone present-ing Clifton with a car. I had to make up for all my recent absences. Was I wrong for pretty much calling her out as a liar in front of Jerald, Linda, and even my son? In some people's opinion, yes, but in my own, not at all. I was getting tired of playing games and going around in circles like we were happy when we were not. Our marriage had gone through the trenches and would not stand the test of time. The sooner Mary started unmask-ing herself as a happy wife, the easier the transition to my ex-wife would be for her.

"Come on, son. Take me for a ride back to my car. It's parked by the dealership." I hopped in the passenger's seat of his new ride.

"All right, Ma. See you later, and don't wait up or wor-ry. I have every intention of breaking my curfew tonight. Naw, I'm just playing around. I'll be there almost on time."

Like father, like son. "Yup, don't wait up for me either, Mary." I chucked up the deuces as Clifton sped off with me riding shotgun.

Chapter Two

Charles Bivens

Mary must have put something into the universe because the mainframe system ended up crashing at my job. The entire staff of computer engineers and technicians were working to get the system back up and running. I was beyond tired from partying all night at the Gentleman's Spot with one stripper after the next, but responsibilities called.

I was about to leave the club with a dancer when I got the emergency alert that the system was vulnerable. I was a computer and electrical engineer. It was my job to not only develop hardware and software for computer systems but to service and protect them as well. I was paid and worth every penny of the $100,000-plus salary I brought home.

Not only was I employed as the leader of a tech team of a mortgage company, but I ran my own business simultaneously. Being able to build and monitor databases for multiple companies via remote desktops and mirroring made it easy to collect several sources of income at once. The money I collected from contracting my services out on the side went into a private account that only I had access to. That's right, only me. I didn't care how many times Mary whined or pouted about not knowing exactly how much I had saved there. That was my personal business. I ensured her and my children were good and that was all that mattered.

My eyes were hurting from scanning the system trying to detect exactly where the network was vulnerable. A computer engineer's worst nightmare was to have secure and private data leaked on their watch. A breach in my company's system of that magnitude would most definitely cost me both my career and my profession. I was working under pressure and trying not to fold.

"Hey, Charlie," my secretary greeted me, coming into the network closet I was tucked away in. "I brought you a cup of green tea, some crackers, and a few Tylenol tablets to help you shake your hangover faster. I know how it is."

"Thank you, Kandace. I most definitely need my head to stop spinning and some food on my stomach. My brain is working on overdrive trying to figure out how to fix and secure this damn system." Taking the mug of tea, I took a few gulps and then swallowed down two pain tablets. "Whoever compromised it, they're very technologically savvy and need to be on our team. They screwed us over big time."

"Wow." She shrugged her shoulders, then stood behind me and starting rubbing mine. "You have to relax, Charlie. You know I don't like it when you underestimate yourself. You got this; no worries. Just chill out."

Her sweet perfume filled up my nostrils, and her gentle touch brought a overwhelming calmness to the anxiety going on within me. For a brief second, I thought about how Mary once had the same power over me. "Yeah, you right." That moment ended as soon as Kandace started speaking again. She had been taking my wife's place in a lot of ways.

"Don't give them that much credit, Charlie. I'm sure you are more stressed and flustered from having to work against the clock than they are smarter or savvier than you are. And I'm more than sure you'll have everything fixed back to how it supposed to be in no time so we can go celebrate. I believe in you, baby."

"I appreciate the pep talk and pick-me-up package." I thanked her, putting my hand up to rub hers then back down on my keyboard just as quickly. I was working like a savage and trying to remain focused, but Kandace's touch was starting to arouse me. She knew exactly what she was doing.

Leaning down and kissing my neck, she then ran her hands down my chest to the rise in my pants. "You are very welcome, boss. Is there absolutely anything else I can do for you? I'm more than willing to work all this tension up out of my friend," she purred seductively, squeezing my hardened manhood.

"Come on, baby." I moved her hands back up, knowing I would not be able to keep my pants zipped too much longer with her rubbing on me. "You know I can't give you this dick or get a treat until my work is done. Stop teasing ya mans. Time is money, and I'm losing a lot of it each second this system is down." The account that had crashed also paid me an additional percentage on top of the company's cut because I was supposed to be the best in the game. This slip-up was making me look extremely bad and could cost me future accounts. This breach was bad, to say the least; very bad.

"Okay, I'll back up if you promise to celebrate with me after you prove me right."

"That's just the right amount of motivation I need to keep my head in the game. I promise you that rain check."

"I hope you didn't call yourself calling my bluff because I was in fact very serious, Charlie. You might as well call your wife right now and tell her you aren't coming home."

Kandace's model-type legs walked out of the network closet. Her sexy ass was a prime example of what a slim, thick chick was. From her voluptuous breasts down to the juicy cheeks I loved to watch jiggle, her body was banging. There ain't nothing like getting a firm grip on her waist when I was grinding into her guts from the back. I couldn't wait to celebrate inside of her.

Kandace had been my secretary for past year. I hired her through a temporary agency after going through two other girls who were good at sucking dick but not good at reception work. I'd needed a woman who knew how to balance both. Kandace could suck me off in ten minutes and write it on her time card as a bathroom break. She got so good at juggling all of my needs that I made her my personal secretary for my side hustle as well. Though Kandace was a more vibrant, wild, and freaky being than Mary, she reminded me of her because they both got shit done. Mary knew how to efficiently organize and execute without a hint of guidance. That was why I was certain she'd bounce back on her feet after the divorce.

I tapped my manhood back down. She'd worked me up and aroused me to the point of me wanting to call her back in for a quickie. I didn't put any woman except for Melissa in front of my money, not even Mary, and she'd invested more than time but years into me. In this hectic situation, I couldn't let my dick do the work for me. I hated and loved my profession at the same time.

It took two pots of coffee and five additional hours of me sitting in the same spot staring at several computer monitors to get the system back on track. I then stayed an additional two hours to make sure everything remained up and running perfectly, and installing additional spyware and anti-malware. It was already bad enough that a security system I designed was hacked. I couldn't let it happen again within the same twenty-four-hour time span. Not if I wanted to continue having a successful career.

Once I reported back to my employers that the system was restored and was back getting praised, I packed up all of my personal equipment and went trucking down the hallway in search of Kandace. With all the frustration, anxiety, and pressure I'd been under trying to fix what was broken, I was eager to have a few drinks and even more eager to dip down deep inside of her.

She had been my personal play toy for the last eight months. I usually did not keep side chicks, tricks, or spare women around for longer than a month at time, if that. But Kandace did not become clingy after our first few encounters and had played a vital role in keeping the glue to my marriage adhered. She made sure Mary got a birthday gift, an anniversary token, and even flowers for an apology after I spent the weekend away from home spoiling her. She kept it professional when necessary but slutty when required. It was like having my cake and eating it, too. I was more than ready to inhale a fresh breath of air and to see what she had in store for me.

"Hey, sexy." I walked up behind her, hugging her tightly, sliding my hand down and cupping her breasts. "I'm glad that you're still here. I know your fine ass would rather be in the club or out somewhere with your girls."

She purred and lifted her head up, meeting my lips for a quick kiss. "The turn up with you is much better than with my girls, babe."

Pecking on each other's lips a few more times playfully, I then tugged on her ponytail so her head would snap back some. She loved it rough, and I liked giving it to her rough. "Gimme that tongue," I quietly demanded.

"I'm just glad you didn't try sneaking out on me and home to your wife."

"You know better than that, Kandace. If I give you my word, then you have my word. I am all yours tonight." I spun her chair around so she could face me.

She smiled seductively, fluttering her eyelashes at the same time. She then started yanking on the collar of my shirt and then ran her finger down the trail of buttons that lined my chest. "Say it again. All mine?" She rubbed on my manhood.

The mere graze of her hand had my manhood hardening. I was tempted to back her up into the janitorial closet, or even up against the wall. I would have done so if the building were empty. I had done so, matter of fact. Kandace and I had screwed all over this office building.

"All yours." I said the two words as slowly as I could so she could hang on to them and believe me. "And if you do that nasty shit again, I will not be taking you anywhere but to the liquor store for a bottle and back to your spot." I was horny and ready to devour her.

Cupping my dick in her hand through my pants, she massaged it and then let it go. Another tease move. Whether she was working toward another pay increase or a free paid day off, Kandace was going to rightfully earn it. She had never been afraid to get scummy.

Trailing behind Kandace's car, we finally pulled into the parking lot of some bar far out of the way. It was seemingly located for people trying to be discreet. I could tell by the way the entrance was dimly lit that I was going to like this place.

Once inside, the lighting did not change much. In fact, it appeared to get darker. Strangely as the smooth sounds of jazz music vibrated off the walls framed with pictures, my hook-up started to repeatedly twitch. I got chills. I was having flashbacks of White China's touch. I knew I was wrong and should have been focusing my attention on Kandace, but what can I say? The dick wanted what the dick wanted.

Soon I was snapped back into reality. As the waitress ushered over to a small booth near the back, Kandace reached back, firmly grabbing my hand. Behaving as if she was marking her territory, I grinned, still finding time to glance at a few nice-looking women we passed along the way.

"You see something you like back there? Maybe one of them old bitches you think can suck you off or take it ball-deep in the ass like me?" Kandace was questioning me as if she were the police or, worse than that, Mary.

"Look now. I didn't come here for all that. I thought we were here to relax, get some drinks, and cut loose. I mean you did promise me if I didn't go home you'd make it worth my while? Now correct me if I'm wrong, but you did promise me a good time right?" I gave her a long, cold, deep stare directly in the eyes.

I was not a rookie with playing mind games with females. I had been manipulating them since I was my son's age. Women, no matter what race, color, or creed, wanted the same thing: to be heard and valued. So guess what I learned. I realized doing just that, throwing the ball in their court and letting them decide where the relationship would go, was key. If they told me to go, I'd get up and head toward the door. Most women say "go" but honestly mean "please stay, kiss my ass, and fight the good fight." Kandace was no different. If she was having a problem with me, I could rise and fly. "Matter of fact, I don't want to have any issues with you and me because you think I want someone else. I'd rather we just end this and still remain friends."

The look on Kandace face was priceless. Once again I had successfully flipped the script. Watching the small tears start to form in the corner of each of her eyes, I started to temporarily feel bad for her. She was definitely out of her league when it came to mind games with the opposite sex. Although she was like Mary in a lot of ways, this was not one of them. Mary was like me. She could smell bullshit coming from a mile away.

"Nooooooo, Charlie, please don't go. I didn't mean to bug out. It's just we rarely get to be together outside of the office, and I guess I want all your attention on me," she pleaded, and I knew I had her back in the palm of my hand, just where a side chick jump-off needed to be.

Two or three stiff drinks later, Kandace was damn near on the sticky floor of the booth in between my legs, craving to suck my dick on the spot. The waitress returned with the bill grinning at Kandace's eagerness. I could tell by the way she kept peeking she hoped to get a quick glimpse of what I was working with. Me being the dog I was asked her what time she was getting off. Busy licking the material separating her lips from my dick, Kandace didn't seemed to care. She was being submissive just like I wanted my women to be.

Chapter Three

Mary Bivens

I was standing in the mirror with the glass of white wine in my hand I was guzzling to get inebriated. I didn't have anything else to do and was feeling sorry for myself. Clifton was out for the second day in a row breaking his car in, which I was still pissed about because Charles hadn't told me he was purchasing it for him. And though Melissa promised to spend some time with me watching movies today, her boyfriend decided to take her on a date. My daughter was getting action, but I wasn't. I was reminded more and more each day of what my future would hold, and I didn't like it.

Waiting for Charles to pull into the driveway last night, I paced the house until my feet hurt. Every horn, headlight, or engine I heard coming up the street I thought was him, so I ran to the window. I wasted all of my energy gearing up for an argument that never happened because he never brought his ass home. I had not laid eyes on my husband since he rode away in the passenger's seat of Clifton's car with his eyes glued to mine through the side mirror. I felt dumb for even caring, but I cared. I was holding on to hope that things would turn around.

On another pace mission throughout the house, I heard Clifton's television playing from in his room. I started to call and give him a read about running up the electricity bill, but I caught myself because it felt like I was being nitpicky and petty. Charles had my feelings all over the place, and I was about to take my anger out on the kids. That in itself pissed me off more.

Clifton's room was a junk emporium. There were clothes, shoes, more clothes and shoes, dishes, and trash all over the floor. I was pissed because he hadn't been raised to be a slob, but I still didn't call. I was letting him have his freedom because it was going to be a different story later. Grabbing a trash bag from the kitchen pantry, I tossed out all of the trash and took the dishes to the kitchen. I then started to put the dirty clothes on his floor into piles. That was when a joint fell from one of the pockets of his pants.

I didn't call Clifton and ask him a million questions or make him come home. I took the joint downstairs to the stove, lit it off the eye, and then smoked the whole thing down to a nub. I felt more jittery and restless than a head high, but still, I felt super good. As soon as my stomach grumbled, though, I remembered why I stopped smoking marijuana in the first place, which was because the munchies made me eat too much food and gain too much weight. Grabbing the keys, I rushed out of the house with my phone to my ear calling the You Buy We Fry chicken spot to put my order in.

Back home, I couldn't get the Styrofoam container of chicken opened up quick enough. The aroma kicking from it had made me hungrier the whole ride home. I was smashing when Charles called.

I answered and cut straight to the chase. "What time shall I expect you home?"

"It won't be tonight so stop calling my phone. You're going to force my hand to add you to the block list, and I don't want to just in case there is an emergency with the kids."

"Are you serious with me right now, Charles? Are you not coming home for real?" I yelled my questions into the phone. "Why are you doing this to me? To us? To our family?"

In response to my questions, he coldly disconnected the call. He had not argued or reasoned with me; and what hurt the most, he was not affected by the pain I know he heard in my voice. The man I had been married to for twenty years had become mute to my feelings. My cries fell on deaf ears. It felt like I couldn't take in any air. It felt like my lungs were going to collapse. I was even starting to feel lightheaded. Shoving the Styrofoam box of chicken off the bed, the rest of the pieces fell to the floor. He'd ruined my appetite.

Hitting the redial on my cell's screen, I was fixing my mouth to curse him out, but his voice-mail popped on. That made me angrier.

"You have reached the voice-mail of Charles Bivens—"

Before the greeting could play itself through to the end, I pressed one to go straight through to his voice-mail. His voice was making my stomach twist up into knots. I shouldn't have been upset, hurt, or even surprised by him telling me he was not coming home for another night. Charles had been unhappy. We had been unhappy. He had been cheating on me for years.

Hanging up instead of leaving a message, I was crying too hard to even formulate a sentence.

I was bubbly and overjoyed on the day Charles asked me to be his wife. So much so that I'd given up on all of my dreams to give him all of his. I was twenty-two years old, fresh out of college with a bachelor's degree in business, and determined to have it all. Despite all the warning signs and horror stories people told me to be fearful of when it came to marrying young, I ignored them because you couldn't tell me Charles wasn't my forever after. He was twenty-nine, already established within his career, and he romantically whisked me off my feet each and every day until I met him at the altar to wed. I even stumbled on my own two feet walking down the church's aisle. In such a rush to get Charles's last name, I never thought once about what I was giving up. In hindsight, I thought that maybe God was sending me a message of what was to come. I'd been tripping, tumbling, and falling down over Charles since that day.

Getting married to him and then having children at a young age kinda put a spin on the ten-year plan I'd plotted out for myself before graduation. It went from being on the fast track to being on bed rest due to pregnancy complications with my first child. I spent all of my hours in that bed making vision boards and extravagant business plans that even included marketing ideas. You could not tell me that I was not going to bounce back from a high-risk pregnancy and get right back into the swing of things.

Well, life ended up proving to me that I should not plan for shit but to take the cards I was dealt. I went from working toward my own dream of being a business owner to only focusing on Charles and supporting his dream from behind the scenes. I had given him twenty years of my life, two kids, and was carrying the burden the heaviest over miscarrying, all for him to basically be saying "fuck you" now that my head was out of his ass. I was mad as hell.

Calling my best friend, I needed to vent.

Jillian and I had been best friends since college. We both received scholarships from a minority organization on campus that dedicated their time and expertise to help all of the African American kids excel. We were counseled and given positive outlets and reinforcements and had a place on campus that was strictly for us to mingle at so we did not lose our black identities while attending a majority Caucasian school. I was very thankful for that society and all of its affiliates each of the four years I was in school. I made some great connections, but none more valuable than the bond I had with Jillian Greene. She and I shared more secrets than some people did with God.

She answered on the fifth ring and barely got to say hello before I started pouring all of my problems out.

"Mary, seriously, girl, please tell me why you are holding on to your marriage. All Charles does is disrespect you. He doesn't even appreciate all the time, effort, and love you put into him. Stop wasting your time worrying about him and find you someone else. Clifton and Melissa are grown now, and have been grown."

"Wow, do you think you could put your guns up?" I wiped at my eyes with some crumpled-up Kleenex. "You're reading the shit out of me."

"Yes, I am. And no, I cannot. As your friend, you need me to be brutally honest with you. I think that's why you called me in the first place. Because you know I'll tell you like it is."

"No, Jillian. I need you to make me bowls of ice cream, watch reality television, and let me cry on your shoulder until Charles comes home."

"Oh, my bad. What time is he coming home? That's right. You don't know if he will this time."

Regardless of my tears, Jillian was cutthroat. I wasn't mad at her, though, because she was right about why I'd called her. I'd needed to vent, but I'd also needed the truth. Jillian had never been able to sugarcoat shit, and she only knew so much about my relationship because I used her as a sounding board. Jillian knew secrets of mine that should have been sacred.

"Listen, sis, I swear I'm not trying to kick you while you're down, but you need to stop letting Charles run over you. You were whole before you met him, and you can be whole again," she said, trying to make me feel better about myself.

"How, Jillian? How am I supposed to be whole without my husband? What do I have that is mine? Everything I have is either loaned to me by him or shared." My truth sounded pitiful. "Who in the hell wants a washed-up housewife?" I felt defeated.

"Girl, why don't you start the healing process off by wanting yourself instead of that no-good nigga of yours you love calling your man? Harsh, I may be. But a liar, you know I am not. I only want what's best for you at the end of the day."

"I know." My voice was barely audible as I wiped at my tears.

"I'm not trying to make you cry, Mary. It's just that I haven't seen you love yourself in a very long time and it's long overdue that you start back at doing so. Get a haircut, go to church, or enroll back into school. I don't know, find yourself some peace and don't share it with anyone. You owe it to yourself to be selfish to everyone else you've given all of your time and energy to for all of these years. Even if I'm on that list."

I fell quiet, taking a few seconds to play back all of what she'd said. "You know what, Jillie? Your delivery might've been a tad fucked up, but your advice was actually pretty good. You are right. I do need to start taking more responsibility for my happiness. "

"Yup, you're damn right that you do." She started clapping loudly, being overly dramatic. "I miss my best friend."

I smiled through the tears. "I miss you too. I'm going to hop on a plane and come visit you soon."

"Honey, yes." She got excited. "I know you're joking, but you really do need to hop on a plane and come to Cali. A little fun in the sun will definitely wake you up from that nightmare you've been living with Charles."

Jillian had been trying to get me out to California for years. Too busy living carefree, she moved after we graduated and hadn't looked back since. I hadn't been since

Charles and I took the kids to Disneyland when they were small.

"I'm gonna show you who's playing once I get Clifton across the stage."

"Okay. We'll see." Her voice was comical. "Let me know what terminal you're flying into, and I'm there."

The conversation lightened up, and we began talking about things with no substance like what was on television, what books we'd read lately, and trivial gossip that was going on within the blogs. I was not savvy with navigating social sites, so Jillian was telling me all the juicy stuff she had read online. She even talked me into signing up for an Instagram page so I could follow some of the pages she was following, claiming that all the comical stuff on the site would help keep my mind busy. So tired of being sad and crying, I jumped on board with her suggestion and even asked her to tag me in posts she found that would make me laugh. I was trying so hard to find a focus outside of Charles.

"Sis, I'm sorry, but let me call you back tomorrow. The young and tender I was telling you about earlier just rang my doorbell."

"Oh, my God, you are a mess. I cannot believe my best friend is a cougar. Some boy's momma is gonna be at your door one day behind their son."

She started cackling. "You might be right about some stuck-in-the-mud momma being at my door because I keep me a young'un. Hopefully, you're here when they do so you can stall them," she said, taking a playful jab at me.

I hollered, "You're silly as hell, Jillie. If I'm an old hag, so are you because we're the same age. So boom and bye."

"See, to further prove my point, your old ass said 'boom.' No one from the younger generation would even know what 'boom' is supposed to mean." She kept taking jabs at me that were all in fun.

I was choking on my laughter. "I can't keep up with you."

"You can, have, and you'd better. You know how we do it."

"Without a doubt I do. I'll talk to you tomorrow. Make sure you make that young'un strap up so I don't have to help you raise no damn kids, Jillian." I sounded like a mother.

She hollered just as loudly as I had a few seconds ago. "Yeah, I cannot wait until you fly down here so we can kick it like back in the day. I love you, sis."

"Yeah, yeah, yeah. I know, and I love you too. Now go open the door for your jail bait before someone calls the cops on you. Besides, you know kids these days have a short attention span. His ass might not even be at the door anymore." I couldn't resist getting a few jabs in of my own.

"All right now, Mary. You better hit me with the comebacks." She acknowledged my wittiness. "But you were right, so bye." She disconnected the call.

Hanging up the phone, I felt ten times better than I had when I picked up the phone. Jillian was as crazy as they came, but I loved her to death. If it hadn't been for her, I probably would have taken a few more antidepressant pills and drunk another bottle of wine. She had no idea that our conversation did more than pass the time, but saved my life.

I woke up to the sound of music blasting outside of my window. The bass felt like it was vibrating the whole house. Looking at the clock, it was a little after three o'clock in the morning. My head felt a little groggy from all the crying, yelling, worrying, drinking, and taking medication I'd done; but I still got out of bed to check things out. The reason why Charles and I had the front room was to watch what went on out front. I was hoping it was him in the driveway.

After turning the light off, I peeked out the blinds and saw Clifton and Melissa coming home. I wondered how they got together, but I wasn't about to ask unless they came to me with it. Jillian's voice kept playing over in my head that I was going to have to start letting them go and grow, which made sense, so I was trying to start. I didn't want to end up a cougar, but I really didn't want to end up an old hag. They were in one piece and together as brother and sister, so I took solace in that and fell back. Jillian would have been proud.

On the flip side, I was upset with myself for jumping the gun and thinking it was Charles coming home. I didn't know why I kept filling myself up with hope that our marriage was going to last when his actions kept showing me that it wouldn't. Quickly slipping underneath the covers and flipping off the television off, I played to be asleep. I was taking another part of Jillian's advice, which was to take some time to myself. I didn't want the kids bothering me.

I lay in bed playing a game on my phone trying to keep my brain idle. The kids had come in the house quietly and retired to their bedrooms. Melissa was in a rush to get out of the house but all but threatened me and her father bodily harm if we changed her room into a den. Though we'd laughed off her request, nothing had changed.

When four o'clock in the morning struck, I couldn't help calling Charles's phone. I was wide awake and felt I had the right to know his whereabouts. My heart dropped when it rang. That meant he'd powered it back on. After going to the voice-mail twice, I called back a third time and the phone picked up. My heart sank again.

"Charles? Hello?"

He didn't respond.

I pulled the phone back from my face, looked at the screen, and saw the timer still counting, and then spoke into it again. "Hello. Charles?"

After a few seconds more of silence, the phone hung up. By the time I'd called his phone back, it was back off because the voice-mail kept coming on. Had I not been high off pills and buzzed off wine, I would have gotten in my car and tried tracking his doggish ass down. When he first started cheating, I used to stay prepped to pop on him and a home-wrecking bitch.

I would follow Charles to their houses. Each time he called himself sneaking out of our home in the middle of the night like a burglar, I had to slow down my movements from beating him out of the house. I would play asleep until I heard the front door close, then hop up already in my clothes because they stayed strategically laid out. I didn't even take naps without my keys being either underneath my pillow or in my pocket. I had been done with chasing him around the city, however. If only I could stop caring as well.

Tears started flowing out of my eyes like a waterfall; then I started hyperventilating. It felt like the walls within my room were closing in on me. Knowing that a full-blown panic attack was nearing, I pulled my depression medication from my purse and swallowed four pills from the bottle with an entire glass of wine. I wanted to pass out. I was tired of hurting. The pills usually helped put me into a careless trance, one where I could take a million gut-wrenching blows and still stand emotionless. I was hoping and praying that an overdose would put me into a fixated one. I wanted to permanently check out of this hurtful-ass reality. I really didn't want to wake up. I hated that things couldn't go back to how they used to be. I was unsure of how much more my heart could take.

Chapter Four

Mary Bivens

"Mom, are you up?"

I lay still and silent, thinking Melissa would shut the door and go on about her business, but she didn't. Instead, she came into the room and opened up my blinds. I was usually ecstatic about her spending the night at home but, right about now, I just want to be pitiful alone. I was too embarrassed to want a pity party.

"Mom, it's a little after ten. It's time to wake up," Melissa said, this time right beside my bed.

"I'll be up in a little while, Melissa. I didn't get to sleep until late, and I'm still tired." I didn't lie, but only told half the truth.

"I know you were up in the middle of the night, Mom. I saw the light was still on when Clifton and I got home, but then it was off by the time I made it in the house and up the stairs. I started to barge in your room then."

"Oh, okay. I didn't know you were a detective. Does that mean you've declared criminal justice as your major now?"

"I haven't, but maybe I should have. That way, I'd know how to professionally find out where Daddy was last night," she snapped at me like a bratty smart ass, one who had crossed the line.

I took three seconds to breathe so I wouldn't catch a case as soon as I got up. Then it was on. Tossing the pillow I'd been holding and crying into off the bed, I leaped up into Melissa's face and reminded her of how to respect me. "You better find your place as my child and rest easy in it, little girl. If you ever stand at my level again like we're equals, I'm gonna knock your dome clean the hell off."

"Wow, okay. Sorry. I didn't mean it like that." Her voice softened. "Let me clear a few feet between us so I don't catch a fade when I tell you this," Melissa said, taking a few steps backward. "Okay, though you just warned me about staying in my place, I really think you need to get pampered and loosen up some. Daddy might not be coming home because you two are always bickering and fussing. I know that's how it is with me and Javion. He always acts funny or stops answering his phone when I get to popping off at him with drama."

"Don't compare your father to some little knucklehead you're dating, that's number one. Number two, I'm not having a conversation about me and your daddy with you. We're mother and daughter, Melissa. Not equals."

"I'm not trying to be on your level, Ma. You keep jumping offensive at me for no reason. I might not be Aunt Jillian, but I did grow up with you and Dad. I know how things were when I was home and, according to Clifton, Dad's starting to stay out more."

There's something about hearing your child tell you that the dark truth you have been trying to hide forever has never been hidden. When I sat down on the bed with my jaw dropped, she continued to tell me things she'd been holding in. Charles and I hadn't been hiding our unhappiness, but making our kids miserable while trying to put up a front.

"Wow, after that read, I think I might need a reminder on which one of us is the mother. Me or you," I spoke from the heart.

I didn't tell her all of the disheartening details of his infidelity, but I did use the subject within itself as a segue into a much-needed mother and daughter conversation.

The hardest thing I'd ever admitted to my daughter was that I was weak for Charles.

As her mother, I always wanted to be the epitome of strength so she could feel strong herself. Daughters tend to mimic what their mothers do. We are their first experience of an intimate relationship, the first person they experience a separation of connection from. I didn't want history to repeat itself with my child. It was my worst fear for Melissa to be a man's doormat like I allowed myself to become to her father. Especially since she was nearing the same age I was when I gave up my life goals.

"So, since you brought up this Javion character, tell me a little bit about him." I was fishing.

"Um, there isn't much to tell except for he's taking classes toward a degree just like I am." She was extremely vague.

"Melissa, what did you just tell me about not being Aunt Jillian? I'm not one of your little girlfriends, either. I want a few more specifics. Is he a sophomore too? What is his major? What does he look like?"

"Whoa, slow down, Ma. Do you want me to ask him for a copy of his license and social security card so you can run a background check on him, too?"

"Well, since you brought it up, I would like a copy of them." I was only half playing. "I just want to make sure that whoever you're dating deserves to be dating you and that you're safe. Now that you're away at college, your dad and I can't properly invade your privacy and boss you around."

"And thank God for that." She sighed. "But look, if it will make you feel better, he is a junior studying to be a teacher."

"An education major? Wow, that is impressive. What grade level is he interested in?"

"High school. He wants to be a college basketball coach one day but knows he has to start somewhere." She spoke like she was his agent.

"Is that so? Does he play basketball on the college's team, too?"

"Yup, he sure does. He is a starter."

"Not that I'm slamming Javion, Melissa. Just make sure that whatever boy you pick is worthy enough to have you." I purposely kept my opinion about her dating a jock to myself. I didn't want to push Melissa away by being overly opinionated and too critical of the company she was keeping.

"Ma, please don't worry about me and my dating life. I don't have low self-esteem, and I'm not foolish enough to get lost in the sauce about Javion or any other boy once they stop checking for me."

If only I could have been as confident as my daughter.

"You've got an hour to get yourself together and ready to go. I'll make some coffee and bring you up a cup."

I wasn't in the mood to get up and leave the house but a spa day did sound good. At least I could get a massage and sip some drinks after a swim in the salt pool.

I took a quick shower, moisturized up, and then dressed in a comfortable sweat suit with a pair of tennis shoes. I didn't even bother adding grease to my hair or edge control to the sides when I brushed it back into a ponytail. My sour mood made it a no-fuss, no-dazzle, and no-makeup kind of day.

Once I grabbed the credit card Charles kept stashed in his nightstand drawer for emergencies, I was ready to go. Melissa might have come up with the idea for the girls' day out to the spa, but her father was going to fully fund it.

"Give me the keys, Ma. I'm going to chauffeur you to-day." Melissa put her hand out.

"Oh, no, you're not. If you want to chauffeur me, you better open the passenger's door to your car. You know I don't let none of y'all drive my car."

"Are you serious, Mommy dearest? You convinced Daddy to let me drive a brand new car off the lot for my twenty-first birthday, and I haven't gotten so much as a ding on it in three years. I can handle your car."

"Melissa, let's not do this. You know I don't have the energy to keep telling you no, but the answer is going to remain no. You're not driving my car, girl."

Without saying a word, she huffed and puffed while walking toward her car. "I swear you're not making it easy to spoil you."

I laughed. "Honey, if this is too much for you, then you better not never have any kids. How do you think you and your brother make me feel?"

She frowned her face up. "Come on and get in before we be late."

As soon as she got in and revved the engine up, her music blared through the speakers, making me jump. It was my turn to frown my face up. "Wow, maybe we should've taken my car."

She burst out laughing. "That's what you get. And since you wanted to be so stubborn, I'm gonna dance and sing real loud. This is what we call rap."

I sat back watching Melissa with my eyebrow raised. When you're young, you never think you'll be classified under the "old school" category. But looking at Melissa was like looking into the mirror at a younger version of myself. Her attitude was ten times worse than mine was at her age.

While she danced and rapped in her seat, I busied myself on my phone. I was looking up graduate schools and bookmarking all the important information regarding what was needed to enroll and the deadline to do so. I was actually starting to feel butterflies in my stomach while researching the programs. Though I'd thought about going back to school years ago for my master's degree, my family and their needs were slated to come first. If I wasn't running in circles for Charles, I was transporting Melissa and Clifton around to all of their extracurricular activities. I'd become an extension of my kids, and Jillian was right. It was time to do me.

A Place To Relax spa was about twenty-five minutes outside of the city. As soon as Melissa pulled into a parking spot, I was out of the car before she was. I'd been cringing in my seat and making faces for the entire ride. The style of music Melissa listened to was garbage. Rap musicians these days only knew how to pop pills and slur their verses.

"Good afternoon, ladies. Welcome to A Place To Relax spa," a staff member greeted us.

Greeting her back, I then passed Melissa her father's credit card, and took a seat on the couch to start completing the health form they'd given me. I wanted to be thorough in listing all of the areas that had been causing me problems. My neck, shoulders, and my hips had all been aching profusely lately. I sometimes couldn't even find pain pills that'd give me relief from the sciatic nerve issues I'd had since being pregnant with Clifton.

"Ma, do you have a preference of a male or female massage therapist?" Melissa asked from the reception desk.

"A female," I responded, almost changing my answer to a male so at least I could've had some strong hands rubbing all over my body. But I was too mad and hurt by Charles to be around a guy. I'd probably end up snapping at him for no reason and not enjoying the experience at all.

"Okay, we're all signed up. I'm about to go call Javion real quick and tell him I'll be indisposed for a few hours. I would have done it in the car, but I didn't want you hustling my words out of my mouth."

"Smart decision because I would have. And while you're on the phone with him, see when he can make time to meet me. If he is serious with you like he says he is, he should want to meet your mom."

She rolled her eyes. I could tell Melissa was swallowing the words she really wanted to say and formulating a more appropriate response that wouldn't get her face smacked off. "All right. I'll be right back."

While Melissa busied herself on the phone with Javion, I busied myself reading the pamphlets they had set out that described all of the services they offered in detail. They had a lot of amenities available for both men and women. In addition to massages, they offered pedicures and manicures, waxing treatments, seaweed wraps, facials, and stuff for couples I didn't bother reading into much because I knew I'd never get Charles out to a spa. I could barely get him to take me on a date to the movies.

My chest started to feel a little heavy. I knew it wasn't medically important like a heart attack, but the mask I had on was starting to come off. Not wanting to break down in front of the other people in the waiting room or the staff, I got up and hurried to the lavatory and rushed into a stall.

It was getting harder and harder for me to contain my feelings. Whereas I've been successfully holding back my tears for years in public, with Clifton months from graduation, the reality that I would probably be divorced within that same time loomed over my head like a dark cloud. Anticipating the storm was killing me slowly. I was trying super hard to kick the foul mood, but the sadness I was feeling on the inside was eating me away.

Tucking my head into my lap, I held on to my knees and rocked until I felt soothed. I didn't want my crappy mood ruining the day Melissa had put together for us. I didn't want to take any antidepressant pills, but I knew I wasn't going to be able to make it through the whole day without them. After I caught my breath and my balance, I dug the prescription bottle from my purse and swallowed one. By the time I counted backward from one hundred, I felt my heart slowing down and I was able to get myself all the way together. I was in the mirror fixing my hair and makeup when Melissa poked her head into the restroom.

"Ma, they are ready for us."

"Okay, sweetheart. Here I come. I'm right behind you." After that mental breakdown, I couldn't wait for the pampering to begin.

The staff member led us down a long hallway into an open elevator, all the while telling us what amenities they had and upgrades they offered. I swear I didn't even feel the elevator move, and the doors opened up to another floor.

"Ladies, right this way. Get ready to be spoiled." She stepped off the elevator and waved her hand outward for us to follow her.

There was soft music playing overhead, low lighting, and a slow-flowing waterfall within the walls enclosing the hallway. I'd gone from dreading having to get out of bed to wanting to spend my whole day getting pampered and spoiled. Especially when we got to Melissa's massage room and peeked in. She'd opted for a male, who were in high demand, so she had to take the spot that had just opened from a cancellation.

Not allowed to take in any electronics, I silenced my phone and locked it away with all my other personal items. I was cool with disconnecting from the outside world, though Melissa had a tantrum about it. She was the popular girl with a flock of friends who adored her. I, however, knew Charles wasn't going to call or check in. I still had not heard from him. Knowing where the thought of Charles would take me, I took a few deep breaths and shifted my focus to something else.

After slipping on a one-piece swimsuit, I ordered a mimosa from one of the waitresses walking around, and then toured the facility. It was really nice and had a lot of amenities. There were a few whirlpools, mist rooms, and saunas, along with a pool that was surrounded by lounge chairs and cabanas. They even had a social area set up that was equipped with a full bar and restaurant. This place felt like a world within itself. I had to admit that it did feel good to sit back and relax.

Thirty minutes before my massage session was supposed to start, I used fifteen of them to wash the chlorine off my body and the other fifteen to just stand underneath the waterfall shower sprout. The water was so hot and so soothing as it beat onto my scalp and down onto my skin that I probably would have gotten off had there been another fifteen minutes to spare.

The person before me ended up adding a few extra minutes to her massage, which I didn't mind because I didn't have anywhere to be. Like I would run home to cook Charles's dinner after last night. He'd have been lucky if I didn't put any laxatives in his meal the next time I did put an apron on in the kitchen. Relaxing in the meditation room, I sipped on another mimosa and flipped through a magazine. I was getting a nice and strong buzz, but I wasn't feeling tipsy or drunk. I'd found my replacement drink for wine.

I was in a zone, a zone that I needed to make my life be more comfortable and make sense. My heart raced as Mahogany came into the room. With a special something about her, she stuck out her hand introducing herself. Her hand felt extremely soft to the touch. I had chills watching how graceful she was. She was the epitome of sexy. Swallowing a lump in my throat, I followed her into the other room, the one where I soon found out the so-called magic took place.

The climate of the serene setting was a little cool for my taste, but I was reassured I would be warm soon enough. With my nervousness, I blushed. I tried to appear as if I weren't scared to death, but I felt she could tell I was shaky. Mahogany gave me a reassuring smile then slipped out of the room so I could get undressed and comfortable. I moved quicker than quick, taking off my robe and getting on the table underneath the white sheet. I'd had massages before, so I was not sure why I felt so uneasy, but I did. Once a few seconds passed, I heard the door open, and Mahogany returned to the room. Her sweet perfume preceded her and filled my nostrils.

"Mary, are you comfortable? Should I adjust the table?"

"No, I am fine. Thank you."

"Okay then. Your massage is about to start and will last for about forty-five minutes. If at any point you are uncomfortable, need a restroom break, want me to apply more pressure in a certain area or even less, please speak up and let me know. My job is to accommodate all of your needs and wants."

"Will do but I am sure I'll be asleep by the time you touch me. I have had a rough couple of days."

"Aw, I'm sorry to hear that." She sounded sympathetic. "Is that why you're visiting the spa today? To treat yourself to a pamper day?"

"Indeed it is, and I plan on enjoying the whole day of services I have set up. I had no idea this place existed until today. My daughter brought me here, but my husband is treating."

"Wow, you have a pretty cool family. That was nice of them." She seemed impressed.

"Nice of her but not of that jerk. He is the main reason for me being so stressed out," I admitted, then felt foolish for sharing so much with a stranger.

"Well, you know what? Let me get to my job of working all of that stress out of you. By the time you get off of this table, you will feel like a brand new woman. I promise."

Starting with my toes, she rubbed and massaged every single part of my body all the way up to my temples. Her firm and gentle grip was perfect. It felt like I was starting to slip into a deep slumber.

Chapter Five

Mary Bivens

"Breathe in deeply and then push all of it out of your lungs very slowly, sweetie," Mahogany softly whispered into my ear. Her raspy voice was calming. "It is never a good idea to hold your breath when a therapist is working on a sensitive area. That is counterproductive and will end up making your muscles tighter instead of less tense."

Keeping my eyes shut, I focused on taking a few deep breaths as she said to do because I wanted to fully experience the deep tissue massage. I was stressed, depressed, and constantly having migraine headaches. I needed this massage to be my relief. I needed all of the built-up stress I'd been holding in to melt.

I was on my stomach, stripped down to my thong panties, and covered in an aromatherapy oil. From the temples of my head to all ten of my toes, Mahogany had rubbed every part of my stress-filled body in an effort to make all of my built-up tension evaporate. It was a good thing I'd spent a little extra time in the shower right before the session. She'd left no nook or cranny untouched.

I especially found pleasure in the massage when she focused on my inner thighs, though. Her strokes on my thighs were long and rhythmic and seemed strategic. It's like they were dancing around with the soft melody that was playing through the speakers. Her fingertips were slow and sneaky, never touching my genitals, but massaging vigorously and rapidly very closely to them. I was trying not to lose my breath, but I was trembling and going lightheaded trying not to climax at the same time. I didn't think I'd ever felt this good with Charles.

"Take a deep breath, hold it for five seconds, and then exhale," she to me to do. "I need you fully relaxed."

As soon as I settled, she massaged from my shoulders down my back and then grabbed both of my booty cheeks. My heart sped up and then almost flew from my chest when she parted them and ran her finger down my crack.

I gasped and moaned loudly, which made her stop.

"No, please don't stop," I begged, not believing those words had come from my mouth.

"I'm going to turn the music up, but I need for you to keep it quiet. I don't want to lose my job."

"I understand and I will," I responded excitedly, feeling myself moisten up at knowing I was about to get touched again.

Dropping my head back into the hole of the table, I bit my lip and took a few deep breaths to calm myself down. Not only could I not believe that I was about to explore freaky shit with a woman, but I was embarrassed of the moans that had already slipped from my mouth. Never ever have I been sexually aroused by a woman, but I felt my clit jumping to this stranger's tender touch. I was out of my element but afraid to get off the table. I didn't want to lose this feeling prematurely. I hadn't felt this aroused in a very long time. Years, probably.

I didn't know how far this new experience was about to go, but I was ready for it to take off. The anxiety was killing me. My nerves were jumbled up into a knot.

As soon as I felt her presence back beside the table, my body tensed up.

"Nope. I said relax." She put some bass in her voice, then pushed down with a little roughness onto the arch of my back. "Flip over so I can work on your front first."

With my eyes closed, I didn't know what was coming. But I didn't have to wonder for long. I felt her fingertips dance across my breasts and then my nipples, finally cupping the fullness of them in her hands until I moaned.

I gasped. I usually didn't like my breasts to be fondled and played with, but she was caressing me so gently that it actually felt good. I was taking note of how she was rubbing me so I could rub on myself. A few seconds later, she started flicking and pinching my hardened nipples with her forefingers until I grabbed her hands and begged for her to stop. "That's too much. I can't take it." My words were cracked.

"Then you definitely won't be able to finish what else I had in store for you to relax."

"Can we try?" I couldn't believe the words had left my mouth.

"Flip back over onto your stomach and let's see."

I almost fell to the floor flipping back over onto my stomach. She slid my legs apart some and then ran her hands down them until reaching the tips of my toes. All ten of them started tingling when she started adding pressure to my calf muscles. Each one of her kneads and strokes was more intense and erotic than last time. I was melting underneath her fingertips. She was far more sensual than Charles. I couldn't stop my lips from quivering.

She then took the initiative to spread my legs a little wider. My pussy started jumping when she started massaging the insides of my thighs with intensity and pressure. It was a mixture between pain and pleasure that felt amazing. Not as amazing as it did when her finger grazed the lips of my pussy and she blew on it, though. The mixture of the hot oil on her finger and her little bit of air made my whole body tingle.

At that point, she'd tipped it to overflow, and I started squirming all over the table. It felt like her fingers were blending in with my skin. I kept tensing up and lifting my booty cheeks up because it felt so good and I wanted more, as I would do if I were with my husband or any man. I didn't even feel like I was cheating and it had nothing to do with the fact that he'd been cheating on me for years.

"Wow. Please don't stop," I panted, pressing my mouth into the pillow so my moans would be muffled. My head was spinning at this chick trying to turn me out. I had never been with a woman, but she was making me want to be.

Rushing out of the room, my feet were not moving fast enough. I had to find Melissa so we could get out of here and go home. There was no way I could sit around here getting a manicure, pedicure, or even relax in the Jacuzzi without me worrying about running into Mahogany again. I had gone too far to go back with her. So now I wanted to run.

I found Melissa in the nail salon section. She was getting her nails polished. I cancelled my appointment before even telling her it was time to leave.

"What? Why do you want to leave? You look super relaxed and like being here is working."

Her simply saying that meant it was really time to go. I needed to be within my own bathroom mirror taking a long look at myself.

"Being here did work, honey." I didn't want to seem ungrateful. "Which is why I'm ready to go home. I just want to crawl up in my bed and go to sleep. That massage wore me all the way out. Especially since I didn't get to sleep last night."

She bought that excuse. "As soon as my polish dries, I'll get dressed and ready to go. The only reason I'm not going to complain about you cutting our girls' spa day short is because we did this on Daddy's dime."

"Good girl," I said. "I'll be in the car waiting."

The car ride home wasn't much different than it was on the way to the spa, except that I was happy to have the rap music distracting Melissa. I didn't want her asking me any questions, and I didn't want to give off the vibe that I was disturbed. I counted down the miles as she drove them, eager to get into my own space so I could process what I'd allowed to happen.

"All right, Ma. I am about to go back to the dorms. Are you good?"

"Yeah, baby. I would not have been if you hadn't dragged me out of the house and to the spa. I appreciate that."

"Aw, it's cool. Don't go getting all emotional on me."

"I'm not. Go ahead and get back to campus so you can catch up with your friends and Javion."

"Bye, Ma," she responded in that "hurry up and get out of my car" voice she had earlier.

Getting out, I waved at her over my shoulder and kept it moving up the walkway. I didn't see either Charles's or Clifton's cars in the driveway, and I did not even care. I had been taking Jillian's advice to make it all about me all day.

As soon as I walked through the door, I started making sure the house was indeed absolutely empty. I went from one room to the next. Clifton's things were all over the house, from the door to his bedroom, and there was a mess in my kitchen from him cooking himself something to eat. But there wasn't any sign of Charles being home. He, however, was the last person on my mind. I couldn't stop thinking about Mahogany.

When I marked the last room cleared, I let out the scream I'd been holding in since I was on the massage table without any restraints. Shouting to the top of my lungs, I stripped down completely naked and stared at myself in the mirror. I could no longer cry victim when I was now a player in the game.

Chapter Six

Kandace Smith

Charles was sprawled out across my bed, naked with his hard meat in his hand. I was about to fuck him into staying another night with me. I hated it when he left me to go home to his wife. Spending last night and the entire day today with him had been absolutely wonderful. He always made me feel like I was his one and only when it was just him and me. I didn't care what I agreed to when I first started working with him; I couldn't keep being his side chick.

I wanted a title more than secretary and some power like a real boss bitch who holds her man down. I made it easy for Charles to make his money so now I wanted to start getting my cut of it. I was worth more than the few dollars he threw me for bills when he fucked, and the salary I got from the company we worked for did not count. I was trying to push a luxury sedan like his soon-to-be ex-wife. Yup, I was gunning for her position and had been since Charles hired me.

Not only did I keep everything running within his tech team operating like a well-oiled machine, I was assisting him on the side with his private consulting firm. I deserved this man. I wanted this man. It was too late, and there weren't any do-overs at this point because his heart was inside of me. I had to have this man.

Charles had taken me on two mini-vacations and five one-night stay-overs, but I wanted to travel the world with him. That should have been easy, too, since if we went outside of the five-mile radius of my home, it was damn near fifty miles out farther, or more, so he could lessen the chances of running into someone he knew. The only reason I was not offended was because I knew my time was coming. Sooner or later, Charles would not have a choice but to let our secret relationship out of the closet. All of my eggs were definitely in his basket.

Me stealing all of his network passwords and paying a geek from his daughter's college to hack into the company's system and break some shit had been one of my craftiest moves thus far. I'd met the kid while stalking Charles. Though it hurt me to see him with his family, I often followed him and imagined myself in Mary's shoes. She couldn't fill them. She didn't deserve them. I was gonna rip them off her feet if she did not easily give them up. Period.

Charles was a good guy, despite the fact that he cheated on Mary. In my opinion, though, he wouldn't even cheat on her if she added some flair and excitement into their bedroom. He hadn't explicitly told me she was boring in bed, but I'd never met a librarian-looking chick who could suck a dick. I was not threatened by Mary one bit. I just didn't like sharing what I loved, and I was starting to love Charles. It was way more than just good sex with us.

Dressed in a sexy lace negligee, I danced over him and let him rub all over my body. I'd put a glittery lotion all over my body on purpose so he would take traces of me home. I hadn't overplayed my position in the past, but I was about to start making myself known as the side chick the closer it got to June. Once he divorced Mary, I wanted to slide right into her wife role and move right into that mansion she cried her eyes out in every night.

When I had sex with Charles, I made sure my guards were all down. Men cheat on their wives with women so those women can fulfill dirty fantasies. It was my mission to be that and more for Charles and I had been. I gave him what he needed, and I was now ready to be more than his work wife. I had a lot of new sex positions to try with him. It was about to go down.

"Bring that fine ass over here, Kandace. I think I have one more fat nut up in me to fill you up with."

"Ohhh, I love it when you talk dirty to me, daddy. You better have another nut for me. Because I've got a lot more juices up in me to wet you up with."

Mounting him so we were face to face, I stuck my tongue down his throat and started kissing him while at the same time rubbing my pussy over the tip of his dick. I was using my leg and glute muscles to keep myself up enough to where I would not slide down on him and cum prematurely.

When I could not take the buildup any longer, I started maneuvering myself into the "rock the cradle" position. Pushing him backward on to the bed, I then put my feet underneath his shoulders, and locked my hands around his wrists and told him to do the same with mine for support. Three deep breaths later, I leaned up and hopped on his dick. He grunted loudly, and I yelled. I can't verbally explain how I felt to him, but to me, he felt like home. As the name of the position calls for, I started rocking back and forth on his hardness, each time his dick sliding farther into my cave. My pussy was sloppy wet and sounding off. When he went as deep as he could possibly go, I swear I heard my back break as I came; then I collapsed on my back fully drained.

"Naw, you are not done. Now it is my turn to put it on you." He took charge, which was the exact trait that turned me on most about him.

Grabbing my legs and spreading them wide, he held my legs down by my ankles and started plunging into my pussy as it overflowed. I was losing my mind. Nope, I think I'd already lost my mind.

"I peeped you trying to throw that pussy on me in a new position." His voice was raspy. "Let me make sure you aren't bored."

Before I could speak up or ask him what he had in store for me, he revealed his plan to me. Lifting up my hips, he pulled me forward placing my feet flat beside him, and thrust into me anally. The sudden and instant impact made me scream louder than I ever had before. He and I had never gone all the way with anal sex, only him playing with my hole at the same time as fucking me and me playing with his when I was going down on him. Me trying to add some flavor within the sheets had backfired on me because he was drilling into me with no remorse. I knew good and damn well Mary wasn't taking strokes like this.

Charles Bivens

Turning the water off to the shower, I took a few deep breaths and let the cold air wake me up. Though I had not put in a workout session at the gym, every muscle and joint was cramped and aching like I had. I was worn out. I could tell from the way Kandace was fucking me that it was for more than just to cum. Matter of fact, Kandace was leveling it up on a lot of levels. I now had packs of boxers, undershirts, socks, and a few work shirts here because of her doing. Since she couldn't put her mark on my place like a typical dating woman could, she was putting my mark on hers. She'd made it convenient for me to stay for the whole day, but it was time to bust a move and go.

"Can you please stay for a little while longer?" Kandace begged, trying to pull my cock from the boxers she'd purchased for me.

"Whoa, slow your roll, girl." I pushed her back. "Big daddy needs a break. I've been stroking you all day and night."

Whereas she and Mary were similar because they could close deals and get shit done, Kandace knew how to viciously break it down on my dick. She was the only black woman I knew who would fuck, suck, get wild without limits, and never put a hair scarf on. Every time I spent hours at a time with Kandace, I always experienced an adventure. But I really needed a break.

"Yeah, I know, right? Hasn't it been amazing? Can't you see yourself waking up to this good ol' pussy and some sloppy head every single day?"

My ear was trained to pick up on a woman trying to get more serious about we were having. My intention was not to divorce Mary and bring home the girls I played with, but to divorce Mary and be free, single, and available to mingle with any and every woman I wanted to.

"What we have works for me. Pussy is always better when you have had a chance to miss it." I leaned in and kissed her lips, then climbed out of her bed. It was my cue to go because there was too much seriousness in her voice. I must've stroked her emotional switch on.

She grunted and then smacked her lips. "Well, how long do you plan on missing it, Charlie? Are you coming back later on tonight?" Her voice was a high-pitched whine.

"Probably not. I haven't been home since Friday and today is Sunday. I have to check in on my family."

"Family?" She sounded shocked by me even saying the word.

"Yeah, family," I repeated myself. "Did you forget I have a wife and kids?"

She coughed like she was choking, but it was really for a dramatic effect. "A wife? Are you for real with me right now, Charlie?"

"I'm more than for real, Kandace. I'm dead-ass serious. Me being over here and in between your thighs does not make me less married. Mary is still my wife, and I will always have kids."

First frowning her face up at the mention of Mary's name, she then rolled her eyes even harder than she had the initial time. I was not feeling the type of person Kandace was transforming into, nor was I attracted to her. I hated having drama, arguments, and controversy with women I didn't have ties to.

"You know what, Charlie? Let me quit talking because it is slowing you up from getting out of my door. I'll see you at work on Monday." Fluffing her pillow, she fell back on it and pointed the remote toward the television. "Bye, and have a blessed Sunday."

I finished getting dressed in less than thirty seconds. "Kandace, I'm going to overlook the tantrum you are throwing because that will fuck up our whole convenient relationship. I don't want things between us complicated or for you to lose your job. When I see you on Monday, please make sure your whole demeanor has improved." I needed her to remember her role and place.

"Yeah, whatever. Just make sure you leave my light and gas bill money on the kitchen table before you go." She waved me off nonchalantly, completely uncaring of my threat.

The money I didn't give her went to China White for a few dances at the Gentleman's Spot. Kandace was as good as cancelled because I did not do drama.

Chapter Seven

Mary Bivens

By the time I woke up from the coma I was in, Charles and Clifton were home. I heard them yelling over a video game. Back when I told Charles I was pregnant with a boy, all he talked about was doing manly things with him. He'd brought Clifton a football, basketball, and Marvel action figures before he was even born. Whenever they got together and played games or sports, it was like two brothers instead of father and son.

I did not run downstairs and jump in his face like I normally would have done. My earlier experience had a lot to do with that. It was after nine o'clock on a Sunday night, which meant the work and school week was right around the corner and regular routines needed to commence again. I, however, was not ready to get right back into the swing of how Charles or even Clifton was used to having things done.

Dragging myself out of bed, I went into the kitchen and prepped a quick meal. I always had food prepped and ready to be cooked on demand because I hated processed foods. Broiling a steak and loading up a mashed potato, I sautéed some veggies to complete my meal and slipped a cold bottle of water into my robe pocket to wash my food down. I wanted to make sure I was properly hydrated since I'd drunk almost an entire bottle of champagne that was mixed in all of those mimosas.

Charles didn't say anything, but I knew he was wondering why I had not called him to the table for a plate but was walking up the stairs with one. I hadn't made enough for him, and I already knew Clifton knew how to fend for himself, so I was not worried about him starving. Wherever Charles ate at this weekend, he could keep eating there. Mahogany had not lied when she said I would feel like a brand new woman. I felt bold, confident, and uncaring.

After stuffing my face, I grabbed a blanket and curled up on the couch in our bedroom to watch television because I wasn't ready to go to sleep. The nap I'd taken earlier had me feeling like I'd guzzled down a Red Bull. After about five minutes of staring at the screen and daydreaming, I went in search for my phone so I could play around on Instagram. I hadn't been on the site since Jillian mentioned it, but I was in the mood for some laughter.

I watched a few videos from a couple of different comedians who acted out skits that she'd tagged me on, read a few gossip blogs, and then browsed the site as a whole to see what else I could find. The more pages I clicked on, the more interesting stuff I found. I even stumbled upon Melissa's and Charles's pages, but their accounts were locked. I didn't want them knowing I had an Instagram account so I didn't bother sending them a follow request. This pasttime was only supposed to be for fun, not a complete time consumer like the kids made it. You had to sometimes pry Clifton's phone from his hand; and Melissa, well, she didn't let you get close enough to her or her fingers if you were trying to take her phone. It was easy to see how the new trend was addictive, however.

I ended up screenshotting some of my favorite posts to put on my own page, uploading a plain Jane picture of myself, and changing my screen name so it wouldn't show my last name. I'd already decided that I wasn't going to be the type of person who uploaded their entire life to the Web. Jillian posted almost everything she did. I spent almost a whole hour alone examining her pictures. The life she portrayed on Instagram looked to be even more exciting than how she'd described it to me the other night.

Right when I was about to doze off, my phone sounded off that I had a notification. I thought it was Jillian sending a message about me being on Instagram, but it was an e-mail with an attached feedback form from the spa. They wanted to know how my visit was and if I would return to their establishment again. Their curiosity made me think of my own. So after I completed the feedback sheet and gave them a five-star review on their site, I moved to the bed and started doing some research on how interested I really was.

The first thing I looked up was some lesbian pornography. Stumbling upon the kinky lifestyle that so many women are obviously living, it felt like I had been hidden behind a rock. The amount of videos that were available and the lewd hashtags that were attached to them had my jaw dropped. Still in all, I was getting horny. It was turning me on watching two women erotically please each other. They were licking, flicking, and even strapping up with what looked like bungee-jumping gear so they could stick one another like men do to pussies.

I never understood why a woman would want a piece of plastic stuffed up her pussy instead of the real thing, until I saw one of the porn freaks going absolutely nutty off of one. It was long, pink, and had beads built into its tip. When I started researching dildos, I learned that those beads were to help women reach ultimate heights of pleasure. I was going to the adult store tomorrow evening to purchase my own play toy to test out.

The more videos I watched, the more I worked myself up. Even my pussy lips started tingling and moistening up. Before I knew it, my hand was gliding down the waistband of my pants and into my vagina. I was turned on enough to masturbate. One of the articles advised that before a woman tests the water of having sex with a woman, she should learn what she likes done to herself. Being that Charles only climbed on top of me to bust his own nut, neglecting all of my needs as a woman, I had no idea what made my body jerk and cum anymore. Other than the touch of Mahogany. I fell asleep touching myself the way she had massaged me onto cloud nine, gently and strategically.

Charles Bivens

"Whoa, you must have really made Mom mad," Clifton whispered, smart enough not to speak loud enough for Mary to actually hear him.

"Why do you ask that?" I wanted to see if Clifton noticed or knew, especially since I hadn't been home since Friday morning. "What do you know that I do not?"

"Nothing. Her and Melissa were gone to the spa and having a girls' day, not her and me. I just said that because she didn't cook dinner and that's not like Mom."

"Nope, it's not, but let us grown folks handle grown folks' business."

"Got it, Pops. Say no more. But about this game, although I'm enjoying tapping ya butt, I need to call it a night so I can stay on top of my game in school. If I slip up once, I know Mom will be coming for my keys." Clifton set the controller down, then stood up with a hand out for me to shake.

"Shit, she won't be the only one coming for those keys. I meant what I said at the school: this car being and staying yours is contingent upon you continuing to make us proud. It is vitally important that you take your education seriously in today's day and age, even more so than it was when I was coming up."

"I'm taking it seriously, Pops. I know I joke around a lot, but I have been seeing what's going on in the news. Trust and believe that I plan on getting my degree and following Melissa right into school. I plan on steering clear of— excuse my language but—bullshit, more than I did before you gave me the car."

"That is exactly what I want to hear. If you're coming out of that same bag on the day you graduate, you might get surprised with some apartment keys as well."

I didn't remember seeing Clifton go up the stairs, but I heard him scream down, "Good night, pops," and I heard his bedroom door slam. I could always bribe my children with money.

Grabbing some ingredients from the fridge to make a sandwich, I made two of them and grabbed a family size bag of chips to hold me over until the morning. I couldn't necessarily blame my wife for being in a pissy mood over me staying out all weekend, but I was pissed. She knew I liked coming home to a clean house and a hot meal. The main reason I got married so early on was because I liked things in my life to go a certain way.

The basement of my house was set up as my man cave. It was my vacation space away from the real world, all of my responsibilities, and anything that required me to think with a sound and rational mind. When I was home, I did not miss a day without coming down the staircase to my sanctuary, most times spending the night down here to keep from arguing with Mary. I did not allow her down here even to clean. I didn't want her stumbling upon some stuff that was none of her business. Even before things between us started being rocky, I didn't share every detail of my life. I got keeping secrets from my daddy. I just had more of them to hide.

After grabbing a beer from the fridge behind the kitchen I had custom built, I got relaxed on the oversized leather furniture I had to pretty much have a wall torn down to get down here. When I got the basement remodeled, I hadn't spared an expense. I had it completely decked out with a high-definition flat-screen television, surround-sound speakers built into the wall, a pool table and dart board to host game nights for the fellas, and a camera setup that allowed me to see what was going on at my front and back doors at all times. I could sometimes get mentally lost when I was in my sanctuary, and it made me feel more secure to have technology acting as my eyes.

Eating the sandwich and chips only made me hungrier. To take my mind off of it, I grabbed by computer and started looking up some porn. I loved sex, but I also loved the anatomy of a woman. When I watched porn, it was not necessarily to cum, but to enjoy the stimulation of it. The most forbidden acts that women do on the videos were the things that turned me on and that I made my prostitutes mimic. I couldn't help my urges nor did I want to.

I skimmed through a few different videos: threesomes, clips of chicks who loved anal, and even a few that had nothing but girl-on-girl action. I fast-forwarded through them, jacked my meat to the best parts, and saved maybe a handful in my favorites file to view later. Being that I was a tech guy, I had a gang of hard drives that were full of porn. Once my dick was strained to the max and the veins were bulging from it, I closed the porn out and opened up the fake e-mail account that I used when I was probing sex sites to hook up with women.

The time and day of having to scout neighborhoods for women soliciting sex was becoming extinct. Matter of fact, unless a person was scouting for a five dollar head job and a ten dollar screw from a dopefiend, they weren't driving up and down main streets in the hood telling whores to get in. Today's technological society made it easy to buy and sell pussy without leaving your home, or from a few swipes on your phone.

I had met girls in hotel rooms, bars, movie theaters, and even at their houses behind meeting them placing an ad on a back page social site. I have spent thousands upon thousands of dollars on one-night stands with chicks off the Internet. Within the last couple of weeks, though, I only spent about a hundred altogether. I was not meeting up with any women because too many news stories were popping up. I did, however, partake in a form of cybersex. I had a few regulars I paid to get freaky for me via Web cam while I jacked off. It was like having a Simon Says sex session. Logging into the chat room of my favorite site, I saw a couple of females I'd Internet banged before were online, and I hit them up. I was eager to start an explicit session.

Chapter Eight

Mary Bivens

I woke up to a cold pillow, which meant Charles never made it to bed. That was not unusual. The unusual thing about this morning was that I did not care that he was not beside me. I didn't even remember waking up last night in a sweat or having an anxiety attack triggered by loneliness.

Resting back on my pillow, I went through my Internet browsing history and cleared all the sites I had been browsing and researching. I did not delete the couple of videos I'd viewed, saved, and masturbated to, however. I downloaded a secret locker application for my phone and stored all the videos and pictures there. I guess I called myself embracing the new me, or who I thought was the new me.

Finally dragging myself from the bed and downstairs, I found Charles in the kitchen eating. "Good morning," he said dryly, only half glancing at me.

"Morning," I returned his greeting, just as dry and half ass. I'd only felt half disrespected when he didn't look away from the television because it was tuned to ESPN, but I threw all of that bullshit out of the window when I saw a dirty sink full of dirty dishes but no food for me to eat. "Um, Charles. Where's my food?" I asked calmly.

He looked up with a stupid expression on his face. "Oh, my bad. I didn't cook enough for you. I didn't know if you

were on a hunger strike since you didn't cook anything
for me last night." He was being petty.

"Stop playing, Charles." I looked in the refrigerator,
oven, and microwave for the plate of food I knew he'd set
aside for me. "Please don't tell me that you left a sticky
skillet of eggs, a skillet of leftover grease from some
sausages, a hard pot of grits, and a bunch of forks and
spoons to wash, but no fucking food. Please do not tell
me that, Charles."

He sighed, acting like he was irritated by how I was
acting. To him, I was sure, I was acting petty, childish,
and immature. But to me, I was being thorough because
I wanted him to realize how hurtful his disregard for me
could be.

"Mary, there is not any food hidden for you. Stop being so dramatic. With all that energy you just used up,
you could've gotten you an omelet going. I said my bad."
Charles was rude and uncaring.

Stomping across the kitchen, I decided to follow his
lead and be just as rude and abrasive. "And with all that
running you just did with your mouth, you should've
been chewing and swallowing. Oh, no, my bad." My
words were catchy and playing off his, but what caught
him by surprise was me pushing his plate off the counter
in front of him.

"What in the fuck, Mary?" he yelled, leaping up, pissed.

"I said, my bad. If it was good enough for me to take,
it's good enough for you to take." I threw his words right
back at him. "Have a good day, Charles. I am going out
for the day." I ended the conversation, walking out of the
kitchen while the final word was under my belt.

I couldn't help but smile to myself. I never stood up
to Charles. But doing so felt too good not to do so again
especially since I knew my switch up completely shocked
the shit out of him.

***

Charles was at work, and Clifton was at school. Normally I would have cleaned up the house and prepped breakfast, but today I got dressed to go shopping. I'd gotten pampered, so it was time to treat myself.

With a coffee in hand, I walked the mall and took note of all the stores I wanted to double back to and shop at. Part of the "new me" plan was to get fit, but I wasn't ready to step into a gym. I didn't know why, but I just didn't like working out around a bunch of other people. That's why I'd ordered a waist trainer a few months back. So I could burn and trim down my waist and hips while doing chores around the house. This is the first time I'd worn it outside of those four walls.

Halfway through the mall, I gave up and got a lemon water from one of the concession stands before heading to the nail salon. I figured I could sip and slim down on an empty stomach while getting pampered. The new plan seemed like a good way to spend my day, especially with thoughts of Mahogany continuously creeping up on the forefront of my thoughts. I was intrigued by her.

Digging my phone from my purse, I went online to her Facebook page and stared at the few pictures I was allowed to see. They were all so beautiful, and of her alone. I wondered if she had a girlfriend, wife, husband, or boyfriend. Or how many people she'd brought pleasure to or confused just like me. So badly, I wanted to see more pictures, posts, and even shares of what interested her. But the account was locked private. What I did know, however, was that her real name was Ebony.

"M. Bivens." One of the nail technicians called out the abbreviated name I'd signed in with on their sheet.

"Yes," I answered, tossing my phone back into my bag.

"Did you pick your color?" she asked in broken English.

"I did." I held up a bottle of bright pink nail polish, going brighter than I had ever gone before. I was trying to be bold and carefree. I was more of an earth tone, natural, calm color type of woman.

With one tech on my feet and another on my hands, I got caught up in shop talk with some of the ladies around me. It felt good being out and about, pampering myself, and having girl conversation. It made me realize how much I had been missing without knowing I'd been missing it. I even realized I had become far removed from a lot of trending topics and that I really needed to get some social site pages. It was odd, and I stood out when everyone started showing memes and videos to one another for laughs.

Once my nails and toes were done, designed, and dry, I hit the mall running. Being that I hadn't shopped for anything more than slacks, blouses, ball gowns, and cocktail dresses, I really didn't know how to pick stylish yet sexy everyday wear. I couldn't wait to shop for my own rendition of what the "in" style was, based off a few of their examples. I'd taken a lot of visual notes in the shop of how people were rocking their clothing. I'd even gotten rhinestones on two of my fingers because one of the girls said it would be cute but simple. And it was. I even liked the hot pink.

"Would you like your receipt with you or in the bag?" the cashier questioned, waiting for the register's receipt to finish printing out.

"In one of the bags will be fine," I responded, grabbing the shopping bag full of Bath & Body Works shower gels, lotions, sprays, and candles. "Thank you so much."

Out of all the stores shopped in today, Neiman Marcus, Nordstrom, Saks, and Macy's, I was most excited about the lick I'd hit in here. The whole store was on sale. I had a set of damn near every fragrance, plus some bottles of their aromatherapy peppermint-scented lotions to stay smelling good for the whole year. I even ended up getting the scent I smelled on Mahogany. I was going to use it in the shower once I got home, but in the meantime, to thrive on the memory, I'd sprayed some on my clothes. Had I really been in touch with my feelings, I might've gone back to the spa today.

Whereas I was usually modest and took it easy on Charles's charge cards, I went crazy on them today. If it was a dress, skirt, shirt, panty and bra set, or pair of shoes that I wanted, I didn't question the purchase. I treated myself to the type of shopping sprees rich men's wives did. I even got sized in the lingerie boutique and walked away with enough sexy sets to change up for two weeks straight. I had already planned to come back in another two weeks when Charles's paycheck hit the account.

Famished and damn near dehydrated from shopping, I stopped to grab a bite to eat and something to drink from the food court. I was hoping not to get sick on the garbage they were offering, but I was too weak to be picky. My stomach felt like it was hitting my back. Running from store to store, I had not noticed how hungry I really was. Anyway, after getting a veggie submarine and a strawberry lemonade to wash it down, I picked a booth so all my bags could sit across from me as I smashed.

"Hello. Excuse me, ma'am." A young girl who looked like she was in middle school approached my table.

I nodded and threw my hand up as a way to speak without speaking. I was in mid-bite but grabbed my napkin to stop any food from falling out. By no means was I about to stop eating.

"Oh, I am so sorry, ma'am. I did not mean to disturb you while you were eating."

How could you not have had that intention while walking up on me in a food court? I thought but did not say the words out loud. The girl did not look to be over ten or eleven.

"It is okay, sweetie. How can I help you?" I looked at the stack of flyers in her hand and then back into her face.

"My mommy just started working at the salon in the basement and told me to go pass out flyers to every woman who looks like she needs her hair done."

I choked on my own oxygen. *Did this little heifer . . .* I was sure my facial expression clearly expressed my thoughts because of how she responded.

First she grabbed her mouth, and then her eyes got big as saucers. "Oops, I meant to say she said to pass out the flyers to all the pretty women I see at the mall."

Though I had just been called out by a kid, I could not help but laugh it off. With my dry and brittle hair pulled up into a carefree ponytail, it did look like I could stand a hot oil job and a pressing comb. "Sure, you did, but it is okay, dear." I smiled, not willing to be mean to the little girl. Having a daughter, I understood the smart mouth of one. Melissa used to get popped in her lips all the time behind popping them off. "Can I have my flyer now?" I put my hand out.

"I'm so sorry." She hung her head while handing me one. "Please don't tell my mom. I didn't mean to say that. It just kinda slipped out." I could tell she was nervous about getting in trouble.

"No, no. I will not tell her. Your secret is safe with me, sweetheart. Just make sure you be more careful with everyone else. They might not be as forgiving as me. Okay?"

"Okay." She smiled widely. "Thank you."

"You're welcome. Now, go ahead and finish passing out those flyers."

I watched the little girl's ponytail fly back and forth as she ran out of the food court and toward a group of what looked like college girls. I couldn't help but feel like time was flying past me because it didn't seem like it had been that long ago that Melissa was her age. We used to come to the mall, shop for her a gang of pretty dresses, and then have a small lunch in the food court. I'd completely forgotten about our Saturday mommy/daughter girl dates.

Feeling myself starting to choke up at the thought of my family growing upward and outward, I took a deep breath and an even bigger gulp of strawberry lemonade. I was trying to get myself together and deal with my new reality of being a loner. Instead of using the beauty shop flyer as a fan to cool myself down with, I called the number on it to see if I could come straight down for an appointment. I'd be damned if another kid said I looked raggedy.

Chapter Nine

Charles Bivens

My morning had not started off on a good note with Mary and me arguing, but I was determined to make the best of the remaining hours of my day. I could not let my home life affect my job. That was the way I made money to support Mary's always unhappy self and our spoiled kids. My job and the elaborate salary was also the key to me going to different strip clubs and having my way with just about any woman I wanted. So I knew I had no choice but to shake our dispute off and keep it moving.

Walking into work with my breakfast in hand, I was about to stuff my face. Me being in a good mood, however, was put on hold once I got off the elevator and saw Kandace eyeing me with disgust.

Speaking to everyone on my floor, I singled Kandace out by name. "Good morning. I'm glad to see you at work bright and early, chipper and ready to make a check. I hope we can all be productive today."

This bird, as my son would say, had an obvious attitude. It was written all over her face as she rolled her eyes. "Of course I am. It's not like I've got a super rich husband at home who will take care of me. Or even a rich boss at this point," she announced, talking loud enough where people within the office could hear her.

I was getting pissed. I didn't like women who talked back or employees who talked back, especially temporary ones. Furious for the second time this morning, I slammed my fist down on her desk, instantly silencing her. "Look, I tell you what. Send me the e-mail address to your temp company contact. I'll be expecting it shortly."

Because I had fucked with her mind, I was planning on giving her a small window of time to get her attitude together before actually calling the temporary agency she was serviced through for a replacement. I was going to play everything by ear. Once I put Kandace in her place, today's workday would go better than it did the other day. And as time went on, it did. I was not stressed, anxious, or worried about any of the computer systems I monitored breaking down. Nor was I worried about losing my job. I let Kandace and her drama be the last thing on my mind. I didn't care that she was still very much upset with me for leaving her dry without dick and cash. That was on her. It was not my fault she managed to talk herself out of them both.

I ran a staff meeting for my tech team and presented them with all the information I had researched and gathered since the crash to ensure we did not let the same intruder outsmart us again. We spent a few hours circling over the information and brainstorming on a new system we all felt the company needed. I then took the plan to my bosses and got the stamp of approval. They did not come down on us about the crash but threw money at our department so we could make sure the system remained secured. I made sure my team understood the importance of them giving us another chance and a grand opportunity.

By the time I had come out of the conference room from the gang of meetings, Kandace had alerted human resources of an illness that I knew she was faking, and she had gone home. It was obvious that she wanted to avoid me, so I chose not to call or pop up over there after my shift. We both needed some space.

***

Pulling into a parking spot in front of the registrar's office of Melissa's college, I rummaged around in my briefcase for my checkbook so I could write out her tuition check. Both she and Clifton were breaking my bank account down this week. But I wasn't complaining because that was why I worked so hard. Besides that, Melissa was working hard at pulling her grades up, and I was paying less than I was last year. Hopefully, just the same, as I told her brother, it'd better be her number one priority to keep her head in those books. I would not accept ordinary from my kids because I knew they were extraordinary. I had paid for them to have all the finer things in life and access to best education. All they had to do was use the jewels I'd given them to build their own empire.

The line was out of the building. At the point I got in line at, they had a sign standing up saying it was at least a forty-minute wait time from there. Had I not waited so late in the game to pay her tuition, I could have paid it online or come back. But procrastination, once again, proved not to be the smartest decision. I propped myself up with everyone else and waited in line.

At first, I used the time to look through and respond to all the e-mails I'd been letting build up. I then went on Clifton's school site and checked his progress thus far, making sure he hadn't conned me. I couldn't let Mary find a reason to say "I told you so" about the car. Kandace ended up texting me a few times, but I did not respond. It was apparent I'd made a bad mistake by not making her temporary position more temporary.

Finally, it was my turn. "Hello, I am here to pay this semester's tuition for Melissa Bivens," I told the clerk.

"Do you have her student ID number, sir? If not, the last four of her social and date of birth."

"Wow, all of that to give you guys some money?" I laughed but was dead serious.

"Sorry, sir. School's policy."

"Not a problem. No problem at all." I pulled out my wallet and provided her with the student number and any other information she needed.

"Okay, sir. I have the student's account up. Will you be paying for the entire semester or for the first six weeks?"

"Huh? What do you mean? Is there a new payment policy?" I was confused, only used to paying for the full semester or year at one time.

"No, it is the school's policy for students who are placed on academic probation during that time."

"Excuse me. Academic probation? Run that by me again."

"Okay, this is awkward," she whispered underneath her breath, then took a deep breath. "The school allows those students who are on academic probation the option to pay their tuition amounts in half. The first half when the semester begins and the second half after the midterm is graded and their overall academic standing is then assessed. If the student is back in good standing, the monies will be due immediately. If the student is still failing, they have the option to either continue with payment or drop the class or classes without the failing grade being entered on their transcript."

"Wow. I would have taken a deep breath before and after that long spill too." I tried making light of the situation, but I was extremely irate and pissed.

She smiled and nodded. "What option would you like to take?"

"I'll go ahead and pay the entire amount. Make a note on her account that if she gets academically dismissed, that money is to be returned to her so she can find a place to live because she cannot come home."

After making Melissa's tuition payment, I started power-walking out of the building. She had some questions to answer after I finished going upside her head. Pulling my phone out of my pocket, I was too busy trying to call Mary to notice I was walking right into a woman until I bumped right into her.

She squealed, as my bump caused her coffee to fly into her chest.

"Oh, no, I'm sorry. I am so sorry." I grabbed my handkerchief from my pocket, reaching to help wipe the coffee off of her but stopping because I did not want to touch her breasts. I handed it over to her instead.

"I will forgive you if you buy me another coffee. I am fine, but I spent my last couple of bucks on that coffee, and I won't be shit without my caffeine." She seemed humble.

I got stuck for a moment looking down at her, into her green doe eyes and sweet-looking face. She was very pretty. "Sure, but all I have on me is a checkbook and a debit card."

"That's okay, the coffee stand is only right over there." She turned and pointed, sealing the next few minutes of my fate.

"Well, let's go get you a replacement coffee." I waved my hand in front of me so she could lead the way.

"So, what are you majoring in?" I made small talk.

"I'm working toward my master's in education."

"Wow, a master's? You look so young, like you are in your first, maybe second year of college."

"Thanks, but I actually hate when people tell me that." She was blunt. "I have gone through far too many grown experiences for me to find humor in being compared to a child."

"I'm sorry. I didn't mean it like that."

"I know, and I wasn't throwing you any attitude, only making small talk like you were trying to do."

I laughed, amused by her attitude. "I can tell you're something else."

"Good perception." She winked with sass.

We continued walking and talking until reaching the coffee stand. It wasn't until then did we find out what we had in common.

"So, do you go here? Or do you make it a habit of prowling college campuses to spill coffee on people's shirts?"

I laughed. "You definitely have a sense of humor. But the answer is no to both of your questions. I do not go here, and I do not make it a habit to spill coffee on smart-mouth women." She wasn't expecting my last comment, but I couldn't help myself from saying it. With all the spunk she had, I couldn't help but want to poke fun at her.

"Ohhh, look at the old man trying to slide in one on me. Good one. Good one."

Once the coffee was ready, she took it from my hands and sipped a few gulps. "Yes, yes, yes. What's your name?"

"Charles." I stuck my hand out to shake hers. "My daughter Melissa Bivens goes here."

I should have taken heed to her sly smile, but I didn't. "Oh, wow. Really? You're Melissa Bivens's father?"

"Yes, why are you asking me like that? Are you two friends?"

"Nope. I don't make it a practice to befriend my pupils. Well, she's not my pupil, but she's my advisor's student. I am the student teacher in her math class," she revealed.

"Really? Now is this not a crazy coincidence?" I was not really shocked because the world is super small. "I just left the registrar's office from paying her tuition and found out she was struggling, surprisingly enough."

"Oh, you have no idea how right you are about this being a crazy coincidence," she agreed. "But I'm not surprised Melissa is on academic probation." Her mouth parted to say something else, but my phone rang.

"Sorry, hold on a sec. This is work, and I have to take this call," I apologized, putting my finger up, letting her know it would only be one minute. "Hey, this is Charles," I answered. It was one of the guys on my tech team. He asked me a few questions about the work I'd left him to do and how to fix a few codes he couldn't get right. Once I was done setting him up straight, we got off the phone, and I turned back to Melissa's student teacher.

"Now, what were you saying?"

Taking my phone from my hands, she dialed her number until her phone rang, and then saved it so she could type in her name. "That I've gotta run to class, but you can call me later." She winked and then strutted off.

Looking down at my cell at her name and number, I edited the name from Tiffany to Thad, knowing I was going to give her a call. She was young but older than Melissa and had a lot of spunk, which could keep an old man like me on my toes. I was going to carefully play around if she invited onto her playground.

Finally en route to Melissa's dormitory, I called Mary to discuss what I'd found out regarding our daughter's academic status, but she did not answer. Matter of fact, I thought I heard her click me to voice-mail. I opted not to leave one since I knew she would be home when I got there. Swerving into a handicap spot, I leaped out and clicked on my alarm, unfazed by the campus police being a few feet away. If I got a ticket, I'd just tell them to take it from the tuition payment I just made that was in limbo. Tiffany had been a pleasant distraction, but I was back enraged.

"Who is it?" Melissa's voice sounded out over the intercom, followed by a male's voice who must have been her boyfriend. Javi-something is his name.

On their own, my fists clenched up, and then I started pacing back and forth. I didn't know what father didn't want to keep his daughter away from every boy in the world. I was about to stomp a hole through the pavement. I was already mad as hell at Melissa for lying about what was truly going in school. Now I was about to pop a vessel in my head from hearing that she was laid up with a nigga instead of studying.

"This is your father. Buzz me up right now," I commanded, not doing a great job of containing my anger.

"Dad, I'm in the middle of a study group. Can you come back later?"

"Have you lost your mind or something? You must have. No, I will not come back. Buzz me up right this second, little girl. Or I'm going to have the car company come repossess your vehicle and take it to the impound lot until you get yourself off of academic probation." I shouted her business out loud for the entire campus to hear, wholeheartedly meaning my threat about taking her car back. My intent was to embarrass her since her intent was to deceive me and Mary, plus waste my money.

"Dang, Dad, okay," she murmured, probably mad she had no other choice unless she wanted to get a bus pass.

Two steps at a time, I was moving like a bolt of lightning up the staircase toward Melissa's dorm room. Sweat was starting to drip from my brow down my face, and my adrenaline was racing. I didn't have a woman's intuition, but I had a man's mentality. I scammed and manipulated enough women to know when my daughter was being manipulated in addition to being dumb. As soon as I opened the exit door to the stairwell, I took off running toward her room.

"Hey, yo," I shouted out. "Hold on, my man. Let me holla at you."

Not only did he look my way and look like "damn," but so did Melissa. She popped her head out of her room, eyes wide like a deer caught in headlights, and then threw her hands up trying to explain.

"Dad, uh, it's not what it looks like." She stuttered over her words trying her best to calm me down.

I threw my hand up silencing her as steam came out my ears. I was heated. "Close your damn mouth, Melissa. I will deal with you in a minute about lying but, right now, I would much rather find out who this li'l punk is." Talking to her but staring directly at him, I started loosening up my tie letting him know I was ready for war.

"Dad." She grabbed at my arm hoping to put a muzzle on my verbal attack. "Can you just chill? This is why I didn't tell you about me and him, because I knew you'd trip."

"Is that why you didn't tell me that you were flunking out of school? Huh? Answer that. You are so quick to make a comeback in his defense, make a case for yourself."

"Would you please stop shouting out my business? Please," she cried out, turning around and stomping into her dorm room.

"I will not. I don't give two shits about your reputation around here. Nor do I care about this puny-ass kid who can barely hold his weight up. I care about my money and my damn respect, Melissa. Do you get that?"

She stood silent but with a frown on her face like she had the right to have feelings other than regret and sorrow. Her lips were not fixed to apologize, but to make things worse. Since I didn't want to catch a case that came with a news story that read DAD KILLS COLLEGE KID,

I had to save her from herself and guide the conversation back to where she remembered to stay in a child's place. Both she and Clifton knew that I was the disciplinarian.

"You need to be more worried about how you have tarnished your reputation, your name, and your word with me." I stated all the facts, then turned to face and address her little friend. "And, you. Whatever your intentions are for my daughter, I want them written down in detail and given to me on site the very next time we run into each other. If you don't have it . . ." I paused, knowing he was waiting for me to finish; then I continued. "Well, that's for me to know and you to find out." I left him anticipating the unknown.

Nodding my head, I closed the door and leaned against the wall with my arms folded and my eyes locked in with my one and only daughter. I thought this was the first time she had fallen from the pedestal I put her on as my pretty princess when she was a baby. I was hurt and disappointed. "Money can be replaced, Melissa. But trust, that is something you are going to be trying to earn back from me for a very long time."

Chapter Ten

Mary Bivens

The best decision I made in a very long time was getting a makeover. I was in a better mood, felt sexy, and felt like a brand new woman. I even turned the radio on and danced around the house when I got home and lightly cleaned the house up earlier. I guess that saying "you look better, you feel better" was true after all.

The beauty shop in the basement of the mall had been full of women. It was safe to assume I'd made a good decision and the business was going to be a success. Every pedicure bowl had a foot in it. There wasn't a beautician in the spot without a hot comb, weft of weave, or threaded needle in her hand. Each makeup vanity had an esthetician working hard at glamming a customer up. And every seat in the waiting area had a booty in it. The little girl had been a great marketing idea, and she must have kept her mouth from calling another woman raggedy. I ended up seeing her asleep in the backroom by the time I went underneath the dryer.

Although I'd gone in with the grand plan to get completely made over, I did not want to mess up and have the whole gesture backfire in my face. Charles might have been a jerk, but he was still my husband and my provider and could be very picky and conservative at times. I couldn't lie by saying I didn't have pleasing him on my mind when I sat in the beautician's chair. So, instead of getting my hair boldly cut into a bob and dyed, I settled for getting my ends clipped, and I had them put in honey-brown highlights with a few hints of blond, and wand curls that flowed down my back. Charles liked his women natural. Yes, I said his women. So I'd been growing my hair since we met and hadn't worn a weave ever at all. My curls flowed then stopped right above my bra straps.

I'd waited the longest to get my makeup done, but it was worth it. The artist worked her magic over my bags and blemishes. I walked out of there slayed to perfection. The experience and turnout made me want to get my face made up on a daily basis. I didn't get a lot of bright colors but a face full of natural tones and lashes to make my eyes pop. I was surprisingly shocked when I looked in the mirror afterward and saw a glow.

Dinner had just gotten done cooking and was cooling down. I'd made slamming-ass stuffed peppers that were piled with beef, pork, and rice. I was not a world-class chef in the kitchen, but I knew how to whip up some good food. My dishes were always better than edible, and from the aroma kicking back from the peppers, tonight's meal wasn't going to be any different. My stomach was grumbling from both hunger and anticipation. I hadn't eaten since the mall's veggie sub, so I was about to throw down.

This evening, I'd prepared enough for both Charles and Clifton to eat dinner as well. I figured he might as well come home to a fresh-smelling house, a hot meal on the table, and a diva. That's if he actually came home. I was not expecting for us to have a romantic night, cuddled up and watching movies. But I did want to get a reaction out of him other than a frown. Tonight, I wasn't walking around in a headscarf and pajamas. I'd strategically picked something cuter and more revealing of the body I was blessed to still have.

Fixing me a drink along with my plate, I got ready to retire to the den to eat in front of the television when I heard Charles come home. Instead of ducking off, I went to meet him at the door as usual. A big part of me just wanted to hear him say how he thought my makeover looked, or to see if he even noticed.

"Hey, Charles. How was your day at work?" I came into the foyer speaking.

Engrossed in his phone, he responded without looking up. "Work was work, but it will keep the bills paid." That was a roundabout way of him keeping me in a place. Charles took being the breadwinner of our marriage very seriously, and he sometimes stood on top of his cash when he needed to keep me or the kids in control. I stood there quietly, waiting for him to turn around while catching a whiff of a new woman's perfume scent. No longer did my stomach turn in knots when I smelled another woman on him. I was used to him being a total asshole and all his antics. I had been dealing with the good, the bad, and the ugly when it came to our marriage for years, so just about nothing at all moved me.

His jaw dropped when he finally turned around, and then his eyes got big. "Well, damn. Who are you and what have you done with my wife?"

"Funny, very damn funny." I was only half offended by his off-color snide remark.

"I'm sorry. I just haven't seen you get made up or change your look in years. I apologize if I'm shocked, but I am." He was honest, and I could not blame him for that.

"Well, do you like it at least? I mean, I know I'm the bomb myself; you just forgot. But it's all good. Thank God I love myself, huh?"

"Yeah, you look good." His voice was caught up in his throat as he stumbled over his words while speaking. "You look damn good, mighty damn good."

His eyes were seemingly roaming over every single inch of my body. I felt like he was undressing me with his eyes or as if I were standing buck-naked in the window of Macy's department store. I blushed and smiled, more than satisfied with his compliment. It felt good hearing him say something nice to me for a change, and I was hoping my new look would be enough to keep his ass home. I didn't know why I craved his attention and approval so damn much, but strangely I still did. After all of the disrespectful stunts he had pulled over the years, it was a wonder I hadn't taken one of my good kitchen knives and buried it deep into the dead center of his heart. Any other wife I knew in our once close circle of friends would have done that, or at least acquired the very best divorce lawyer their husband's money could afford.

I heard Charles sniffing behind me as he trailed me into the kitchen. "Did you fix enough for me to eat or am I fending for myself, beautiful?"

Beautiful. My eyes got wide, and a smile spread across my lips at the compliment. I was glad he could not see my elated reaction. "Um, yeah, you can eat." I giggled. I almost forgot he'd asked me a question.

"Good, because the game is coming on and I didn't have a chance to stop and grab a pizza after the drama at Melissa's school. I cannot wait to kick back with my feet up for a few hours. It's been a long, crazy, stressful-ass day."

Everything he said about the game and relaxing went in one ear and out the other. I was only focused Melissa and the word "drama."

"Huh? Wait a minute. What drama was there at her school and why am I just now finding out about it?" I spun around grilling him.

"First of all, I tried calling you but you didn't answer," he defended himself. "Please don't start nagging me. I already told you I'm so not in the damn mood. Now we were doing so well, so don't spoil it with your foolish mouth."

"Foolish mouth? Oh my God, are you serious right now? Whatever, Charles. Now, what in the entire hell happened with Melissa? I'm waiting," I demanded with my arms now folded. I didn't care how much I irritated him.

"I went to the college to pay her tuition and found out she's on academic probation. If she doesn't get her shit together in six weeks, she'll be kicked out." His words momentarily stopped my heartbeat and burning desire to smack the fire out his mouth for talking to me as if I were one of his children or, worse than that, one of his many jump-offs.

"Wait a damn minute and quit making stuff up, Charles. There is no way in hell that girl is starting off the semester on academic probation. She went to summer school and passed both of the courses with B-minus averages."

"There's most certainly some bullshit somewhere in the game then, Mary. And you just made it worse because I didn't even think about her just finishing up summer school for math, or supposedly finishing it up. I'm almost afraid on checking into what really happened during those months and with my money because I might kill her if she's become a habitual liar." Charles's voice was mixed with hurt and pain.

He didn't have to verbally say he was hurt by Melissa, the apple of his eye, for deceiving and manipulating him. I easily recognized it. I was angry too. But I'd already classified my kids by their personalities and Melissa was a lot like her dad. They both could be overly self-absorbed. Charles was getting what he spit out, literally.

"I'm going to call her in a few to see what's going on," I announced annoyed that he knew something before me about one of our kids, then had to have the nerve to be so nonchalant about telling me.

"Well, you better hope she answers and is not cuddled up with that punk, whom I better not find back over in her dorm again or she will be half-ass going to college from this house, and I'm not playing."

"I see you are in rare form today, but please slow down a bit and fill me on what else you talking about." I couldn't keep up with the update on his surprise visit to our daughter's school.

"When I went to her room to check her about lying, she had the nerve to be laid up with some lame nigga."

"Who, Javion? Her boyfriend?"

"Yeah," he grunted, then proceeded to tell me all about the scene he'd created for Melissa to live out each second afterward. Though she was wrong on all accounts for not being upfront about her situation, I thought Charles could have handled it a little differently given our fucked-up marital situation. Being that I knew she and her brother were well aware of me and their father being miserable, I understood why she might've been acting out. There could be so many different reasons and levels as to why Melissa lied. Until I spoke to her myself, I could not go off of what Charles was telling me.

When he saw I was drifting off from the conversation, he came picking at me. Charles knew how I felt about my kids, especially since he was always at work and I was always at home. Stay-at-home parents have different bonds with their children than parents who work full time.

"So, what is your opinion on all of this? What will be our game plan if she does get kicked out of school?"

"I don't know, Charles, but I went through a rough patch too when I was in college. It only lasted for about a semester and a half."

"Oh," he sounded off like was surprised. "What is that supposed to mean? We let her run wild lying and wasting my money going to that expensive-ass college?"

I sighed. "It's not always about the money, Charles."

"Yeah, you would say that since it's not your money being spent."

"Okay, on that note, I'm gonna take my dinner and leave you to fix your own plate. Be careful as to which stuffed pepper you pick because I put a li'l laxative in one of them," I lied to get a reaction out of him. The kitchen was the only room in the house I had an upper hand in.

"Damn, I didn't mean it like that," he tried apologizing. "You know how I get when my money is involved. I don't mind doing absolutely any- and everything for those kids but I will not tolerate nor give wiggle room when it comes to lying and disrespect."

"Funny." I snickered. "You're big on respect but also disrespect at the same time."

He looked strangely at me.

"What that means is that, if you cared, you would know how I get when you throw in my face that I'm only a stay-at-home wife. I do have a degree, you know."

"I know, and since the kids are now about to be out of your hair, maybe you can put it to use. When you were helping me get my consulting firm up and running, you were one helluva asset. I couldn't have done it without you."

"Wow." I was flabbergasted. "I cannot believe you are finally giving me some credit for more than being a damn chef and a maid."

The look Charles gave me made me wonder what he'd thought at that exact moment. "I should have thanked you more for a lot of things you have done for me, Mary. I appreciated them while you were doing them and I appreciate them now, even with us going through what we are going through."

I smiled, not because I thought we were having a breakthrough moment, but because I was finally getting the thanks I had been deserving to hear. "I think that is the nicest thing you have ever said to me, Charles, for real. Thank you."

The door opened and the moment was over. I only got a brief moment to wonder if it would ever be relived.

Clifton walked in. "What's up, 'rents? What are y'all in here doing? Playing nice I hope."

"Hey, sweetheart. How was school?" I asked, poking out my cheek for a kiss.

"It was good. Got a B on my chemistry exam; plus, a few honeys are checking for me," he bragged, sounding just like a seventeen-year-old boy.

"That's because of that fancy-ass car you've got parked in the driveway." I rolled my eyes at Charles. "Don't you let that car get my baby into no trouble with no girls. I might not be ready to have my babies grow all the way up, but I'm not trying to replace them with grandkids."

"Whoa, Ma! Slow up with that baby talk. I don't even want any kids," Clifton revealed, with a disgusted look on his face. "I'm trying to graduate, go to college, and travel when school's out. I don't have time to be changing no diapers."

"Good. Make sure you keep it that way." I nodded, staying firm.

He gave me another kiss on my cheek. "I won't be the kid to let you down, Ma."

"What? What, boy? What is that supposed to mean?" I tried grabbing for his backpack to snatch him back, but he was playfully sliding away from me.

"I'm about to get cleaned up for dinner so Pops and I can watch the game," he sang out, knowing he'd opened up a can of worms.

I looked over at Charles, who was wearing an "I told you so" expression. He cleared any doubt if I thought he wasn't thinking that, and said it. "Check on your daughter and get her together before I do."

"Will do," I mumbled, rolling my eyes at him.

"Now, can I eat for real or were you serious about there being a laxative in one of them?"

I grabbed his plate, put a pepper on there, and then grabbed him a beer from the fridge. "No, I wasn't, so enjoy your meal."

"Thanks. You know where I'll be." He was eating before his feet hit the basement stairs.

Finally free from Charles, I rushed to call Melissa. I needed to first find out if she was okay, and then secondly ask for her version of what happened. I was heated with her for lying about school, but I was not on Charles's side for how he reacted. He was wrong for embarrassing and belittling her. I thought Melissa would be quick to answer, start up a text conversation, or at least call me back. But she did not do any of those things. I concluded from her lack of response that she was still very much upset.

Upstairs in my room, I started trying on all the clothes I'd bought, along with all the shoes, and modeled for myself in the mirror. I absolutely loved my new look. I didn't have anywhere to go in them, but I was going to be cute once I did.

Deciding to take a few pictures for my dull Instagram page, I chose a cute little outfit and a pair of flats, so it wouldn't seem like I was purposely dressing up for the Internet. I then looked in the mirror and fixed my makeup as best I could. I started uploading pictures of my new style; then Jillian called.

"Oh, okay, I see you stunting for the Gram." Jillian used some young-girl lingo.

I laughed and called her out. "Stunting? Who taught you that slang? That young and tender who was over the night?"

"Don't make me block you." She was giggling. "But anyway, let's shine a bright light on your fine ass. Your makeover is cute," she was excitedly complimenting me.

"Thanks, friend." I was sure I was blushing through the phone. "I've been playing by the rules you suggested the other night."

"Hmm, really? And which rule was that? You know I be running my mouth."

I laughed at her comment about running her mouth. "Ain't that the truth? But so was what you said about me needing to focus on me. I've been on the 'all Mary, all day' rule and I'm feeling so much more alive and refreshed."

"And you know what?" she asked but didn't wait for a response before continuing. "You sound a whole lot better than when we talked the other night. Like a whole new woman."

"I do? For real?"

"Yup. You know I don't sugarcoat shit for you. That's why we are having this conversation right now."

"True, true," I agreed. "And, since you brought it up, I actually need to tell you something else and get your opinion on it. I'm about to burst open from holding it in."

"Well, what girl? Spill it. You know I love sipping on hot tea."

"Okay, hold on. Let me make sure Charles is still downstairs." I went out of the room, looked over the landing, and saw all the lights were still off; and then I went back into the privacy of my room. Though I hadn't felt strange being around Charles, I did not want him overhearing what I had done.

I took a deep breath and started telling Jillian everything about the massage I'd gotten at the spa. I told her how the woman touched me, how I had a happy ending, and how I had not stopped thinking about the woman since. I even told Jillian that I'd researched articles to see if I was bisexual or gay. By the time I was done revealing my secret to her, my chest was burning with anxiety wanting to hear what she thought.

After a few seconds of awkward silence and me being afraid to say other word, Jillian finally spoke up. "Okay, I might be a little out of my element when it comes to that subject. I've never been with a woman."

"So? You don't have to have your own personal experience to give me some advice. You aren't married, but you tell me about Charles."

"That's because I've been with a ton of different men. I don't want to give you the wrong information and stir you wrong."

"I feel that, sis. But what would you do if you were me? By you knowing me? Put yourself in my shoes."

"But you weren't in shoes on the massage table," she joked, making light of the situation.

"Jillian. Stop playing. I'm for real." I got extremely serious.

"Okay, if it were me, I would act on those feelings. Hell, I think you should act on your feelings. If it doesn't work out, what do you have to lose? You are forty, your kids are grown, and your husband has been unappreciative of you for years. I'm surprised you haven't been cheating."

"So, do you think I should send her a friend request on Instagram? I found her off the spa's page."

"Oh, my. You really are checkin' for this chick. What's her screen name so I can look at her profile picture?"

I told Jillian and waited or her to look and tell me her opinion.

"I would tell you to fall back with that stalker shit under normal circumstances, but since you two have already gotten naughty, why not? Click 'request' right now. She is a baddie."

Letting my finger linger over the request button for a few seconds, I clicked and held my breath. *Please don't let this be a mistake.* "Done."

"Good. Now, let me know when she accepts. I've got a date with the young and tender from the other night to get ready for."

"Okay, sis. Thanks for the advice and giving me a push."

"You're welcome, but I didn't do anything but tell you what you already figured out and only wanted confirmation on."

Hanging up the phone, I kept refreshing Mahogany's Instagram page trying to see if she'd accepted me until I ended up dozing off.

Chapter Eleven

Charles Bivens

On the car ride home from Melissa's school, I had called Clifton and let him know we needed to spend some father-son time together. He was the one who'd reminded me of the game coming on. He was a sports fanatic but, like me, not a player. We both were avid spectators.

In between watching the game and talking about the plays and the players, my mind kept wandering to Mary, which was very different from what it normally wandered to. I was usually caught up in my thoughts about how Kandace let me bend her over my desk at work, or how China White bounced up and down in my lap at the club. Mary had not given me a reason to give her a second look in a long time, let alone a lingering thought hours afterward.

When the game went off, I stopped Clifton from going upstairs so we could talk. I didn't want to lose my grip on him like I had his sister; plus, I wanted to manipulate him into telling me about his sister. They fought like every other set of siblings, but they had a great relationship. Mary did a great job of making sure of that, and I was grateful. The two of them were from my genes, and they were all I had, which was why I could not let the shit I'd had going on in my life make me fuck up theirs. Melissa had never defied me, or her mom, to my knowledge, like she had been doing since Mary and I fell out. I was an engineer, so it was my job to figure out patterns, consistency, and outcomes.

We talked about the girls who were checking for him, his plans for college and where he wanted to go, and what he might've wanted to major in. For every question that I had, he gave a sound answer. It appeared like he had his head on straight and was on the right path.

"So, what's going on with your sister and this Javion boy?" I bluntly asked out of nowhere.

"Man, Dad. I don't know. I met the cat like twice and wasn't really feeling him. He seemed a little weird, but I shook it off because I have not cared for any of her boyfriends."

"Well, don't shake that feeling off. Learn to trust your intuition in everything that you do. Your feelings about that boy were probably dead on. I met him today and wasn't impressed. He's disrespectful to be all in her room sleeping with her but hasn't come over here to properly introduce himself to me and your mom."

"Ugh, Dad. I do not want to think about Melissa doing it with some boy." Clifton was grossed out.

"I get that. If it were me, she'd be celibate until I picked her husband. But since I can't, I need you to do me a favor and watch out for her. Now that you have that car, pop in on her at school randomly. Ask her to tutor you and then spend the night. The more you are there, the less that Javion boy will be." I wanted my plan to work.

"You know what, Pops? That might not be a bad idea. I can watch Melissa, report back to you for a few extra dollars on top of my allowance, and run game on a few baddies all at the same time." Clifton rubbed his hands together like an opportunist.

"All right, son. Slow down. I am game for giving you a few extra bucks on your allowance in exchange for what I've asked of you. But as far as spitting game on a few baddies go, you better remember what your mother said and don't bring no babies home to this house."

He started laughing. "Don't use Mom as no scapegoat. She might not be ready to be a grandmother, but you really aren't ready to be grandfather." He stretched the word "really." "You just spent the whole weekend out and had Mom crying."

"She was crying?"

"I tried telling you what went on but you told me to let grown folks handle their business." He told the truth. Those were my words exactly. "She always drinks a lot, cries a lot, and paces the floor by the window waiting for you to come home. I know y'all are probably headed for a divorce, but you should speed it up and stop hurting her."

"Damn." I dropped my head. I'd reached the point in my life that every father reaches, especially when he's been out doing crazy things like I had. My son was preaching to me what I preached to him. He was putting me in my place. "I guess I've lost grips on both of the women in my life."

"But it's not too late to fix things with Mom. All you have to do is show her that you care, invest some time into her, and come home. Stop making her sleep alone." It was obvious that Clifton was more in touch with what was missing between me and his mother romantically than I was. I saw that as a problem.

"Oh, okay. I didn't know you had so much experience with women," I joked, pulling him in for a father-son hug.

"I told you the baddies be on me." He laughed and hugged me back. "But for real, Pops, please make it right with Mom. I hate seeing her hurt and I don't want to be in the middle of you two when there's a split. Even if you can't salvage the marriage, salvage the friendship."

"Wise words from a wise young man." I gave my son his props and thanked him for his advice. "Now go on and get to bed so you can get to school on time."

When I was alone, I sat and drank with nothing but thoughts swirling around in my head. I thought about Mary's breakdown in the kitchen earlier. I thought about what she'd said right before Clifton came in about me not appreciating her. And I thought about Clifton said most of all. It's like he'd tied everything together and opened to my eyes to how foolish I had been. My marriage might've had a chance if I gave it a chance.

I drank some more and pulled out my computer. I needed to see if there was still a spark in my marriage before I jumped back into my marriage. And the only way to see that, for me at least, was through sex. If we were no longer compatible in bed, I'd have to do the latter of Clifton's suggestions and work on salvaging the friendship. Being that we hadn't connected like that in a long time, I wasn't sure I'd be able to perform on the spot. To be certain, however, I watched a porno and jacked my dick until it was firm and full. Two seconds later, I was creeping up the stairs toward our bedroom.

Mary looked beautiful lying across the bed, and I was shocked that I thought that. She hadn't changed her look up much in years. I was surprisingly shocked to see her made up today. If we did end up working on our marriage, that'd be one of my weekly requirements of her. Right up there with keeping my meals cooked and the house clean.

Rubbing my manhood, I moved toward the bed and pulled the blanket down her legs. She was asleep in only her panties and a T-shirt. Her legs looked so smooth that I had to touch them. She stirred in her sleep, and then her eyes popped open. "Charles? Stop. What are you doing?" she questioned, lifting herself up some and sliding backward. She was acting like I was a stranger.

"I'm sorry, baby. I'm so fucking sorry for making you think I didn't and don't appreciate you." Dropping my head to her stomach, I felt she was drawn back as I started kissing on her navel. I felt guilt rush through my body knowing I was the reason for her breaking apart. Mary had given me life but in return had been receiving a nightmare. *Yeah, I ain't shit,* I told myself, wanting to make things right even more. Tugging at her panties, I wanted to start working hard on making things right.

"No, please stop. I'm so mad at you, Charles. I think I might hate you." The resentment, anger, rage, and truthfulness in her words was loud and clear, though she was whispering.

I didn't want to hear her feelings nor accept them. I was well aware of what I'd done. "Shh, please let me make it right. Or at least make you feel a little better." If I could give her temporary peace tonight, we could deal with everything in the morning.

Able to get her panties down with her legs spread open wide enough for me to flick my tongue on her clit, I dove in milking her quickly and loving every drop. Panting, breathing hard, she grabbed at my head. I continued to dine on her sweet delight as she ground hard, teaching me a lesson for stepping out on her.

Mary's body suddenly felt an indescribable surge. Caught off guard, her mouth opened wide, but no words could escape, only thoughts. Oh, shit! Oh my God! Oh, yeah! Damn! Shit! *She was out of her mind as Charles's tongue licked her cat as if it were an ice cream cone on a scorching hot summer's day. Raising her head to look between her legs, all Mary saw was the top of Charles's head. Instinctively, her hands reached downward, holding on to the nape of his neck.*

"Umm, umm," *Charles hummed, vibrating her raw walls as his urge became fulfilled. Every motion of him deep tongue-fucking Mary was calculated.* I gotta get her back on my side. I just have to. *Noticing her lower body rise off the bed to meet each wet, long lick,*

Charles took two fingers of each hand, using them to stretch apart her fat, protruding, hairy lips. Staring at her inner bright pinkness in the dim light, Charles's mouth devoured her surprisingly tiny clit. He sucked it gently while teasing it with the tip of his tongue. Mary screamed out his name twice.

"Charles! Ohhhhh, Charles!" Her raspy tone voice echoed throughout the room.

Reaching one hand up, he instantly covered her mouth, still going in, eating her out. "Shh." He came up momentarily for air. "Lie back, close your eyes, and cum for daddy!" When he was sure Mary was going to be quiet, he removed his hand, grabbing her left 36-DD breast. Pinching her nipple, Charles bobbed his head back and forth, his face completely buried in the moist, nappy dugout.

Finally, Mary climaxed the first time, creaming as if she were a man. "Oh, yessss." Exhausted, she tried desperately to catch her breath because it was obvious her once loving mate was not done.

I went back at it as if I were some sort of wild animal in heat. I was acting as if I were a teenager again. I knew my back was going to be sore in the morning, but I didn't care. I had to do whatever it took. No pain, no gain, no Mary.

"Don't stop. Oh, shit. I'm about to cum again. Oh my God, Charles. Please don't stop. That feels amazing."

Feeling her grip my head, I dove my tongue in deeper once more, willing to do anything to keep her from leaving my side. I was giving it my all. At this point, I had no other choice. It was going to be a lot to ask of her to hold me down after all of my infidelities, but I was going to try.

She tasted the very same way she'd tasted, if not better than, the last day I dined on her. Mary deserved a happily ever after for being loyal. Feeling her sweet cum squirt

into my mouth, I bit down tenderly on her thumping clitoris, hoping that still drove her crazy. Coming up from
her warmth, I wiped what was dripping from my mouth
and proceeded to the next step.

With a mixture of Mary's cum-filled juices and his
sweat dripping from his mustache, I stood. Conceitedly
I leered down at a semi-nude Mary sprawled across the
huge bed. Proud I'd made another female call out my
name, I slowly stroked my dick while tugging at my balls.
"Okay, now nasty bitch, play with yourself! Stick those
fingers up in that hairy monkey!"

In the privacy of our bedroom with all the pictures on
the walls surrounding us, Charles shook his Mr. Goodbar,
as Mary once nicknamed it when we first started dating.
"You wanna taste this good dick, girl? You wanna suck
it? You wanna drink this hot milkshake I got?" Tight-
ening my grip, jerking up and down, then down and up,
moments later I shot off a warm stream of thick nut on
Mary's pudgy stomach. I could tell that she would be
back loving me soon if not right at this moment.

I was about to make love to her. Taking my boxers all
the way off, my dick was already hard enough to bang
her wetness out. Sliding in with a little hesitation
from her because her pussy lips were puckered up and
snug, I dug into valley hearing her scream and seeing her
shake.

"I'm so sorry, damn I'm so sorry," I apologized to her
with each stroke, mesmerized by how good she was feeling.

She cursed, cried, and moaned, all while grabbing
my back so I'd slide deeper inside of her. At some point,
she'd gone from fighting me off in tears to being adamant
that I give it to her rough and hard. I could tell she hadn't
been with anyone else because she was too tight and too
hungry to cum. Feeling her legs wrap around my body

as I transitioned from roughhousing her body to making intimate love with her, this was my way of making up my doggish ways to her. Kissing every inch of her body, sucking on her fat nipples, and wiping away her tears, I swirled my dick around in her, feeling like I should've never left.

Kandace

I'd called, but he'd sent me to voice-mail. I'd texted, but he hadn't responded. If I could have, I would've put the Bat-Signal into the air for him to reach out to me. At least then my feelings would have been spared. I had been torturing myself for hours.

Charles has me fucked up. And I couldn't say the shit no nicer. After he left my house without leaving the bill money, I kept waiting for him to come back and make things right and he never did. Then, I got dressed up and cute for work the next day, thinking he was going to say he was sorry and make up with me with a hot session in his office that ended in me across his desk; but that didn't happen, either. Charles actually had the nerve to throw shade at me, and then reprimand me. I couldn't believe he threatened to call my temporary service to have me displaced.

"Stay in your place." His words played over and over in my head like I really had a place to stay in. He'd been made the lines blurred between us. It was killing me that I really didn't know where we stood or where our "relationship" was going.

As the sun started to peek through the dusk-lit sky, I circled the subdivision of where Charles and Mary lived. All night, I had been back and forth between their property and a few other ones around here. I even grabbed some snacks from 7-Eleven and an Extra Value Meal from McDonald's to help soothe my stomach grumbles as I stalked and waited. I wanted to find out what made Charles want to come home. I wanted to find out what made his home so special. And, most of all, I wanted to start following his wife. If I couldn't make Charles leave Mary, I was going to force her into leaving him.

It had made me sick to my stomach seeing them together as husband and wife. I saw Mary greet him in the foyer, and even how he smiled when he saw that her raggedy ass had been cleaned up. I was salty over her looking like a million bucks while I had heavy black bags underneath my eyes and nappy edges from crying all day long.

The subdivision they lived on had a pond, a "playscape," and a pool on the property. Charles and Mary's house was directly across from the pool. I was parked in one of the spots in the lot with my binoculars to my eyes looking into their house. I saw Clifton talking on the phone in his room, I saw Mary dart in and out of her room on the phone, and I even watched her get up in her T-shirt and panties and turn their bedroom light off. I imagined what it would be like to be in her skin.

I knew Charles would never think I'd be outside of his home stalking him. He probably didn't even remember bringing me here when we first started messing around. It was on one of the first few nights of us creeping. We'd been drinking and partying at the company's office party all night and were headed to a hotel for the night when he got the idea to stop at home for a video camera to film us. He thought I was asleep in his front seat when he darted into the house for it, but I was really faking sleep so I could do what I was doing now. I hadn't been able to see his address but was able to pick up our exact longitude and latitude after turning on the location feature of my phone. I guess I knew I'd end up as the bitter side piece.

The house sat still and dark for a while. I almost got bored enough to pull off, until I caught a glimpse of Charles walking through the house. The downstairs light had popped on out of nowhere. My heart sank at how good he looked, especially since he was wearing the boxers I'd bought for him. Charles's body was banging. I even got caught up for a split second thinking about how good it felt being held in his muscular arms.

I grabbed my phone and called him, but he looked at it and sent my call straight to his voice-mail. My heart sank at the sight of him ignoring me, but it completely stopped beating when I saw him go into bedroom and slide those boxers off. "Liar, liar, liar," I cried out, slamming my fist against the window of my car. "I thought you said you weren't fuckin' her anymore."

The keys were in the ignition, but I still was fumbling with them to get the car started. My nerves were bad, and I was moving too fast. It was worse than I thought. Charles hadn't just come home. He was about to cum home with Mary. I was heated. Finally I get the car to start. I pulled out of the parking spot and zoomed around the curves it took to get on the other side of the pool to their house. Parking a few doors down, I cut the lights off but left the car running as I got out. Since the house was dark and I couldn't see with my own eyes through the binoculars if Charles was back to sleeping with Mary, I was going to hear it with my own two ears. Their bedroom window was wide open.

I rushed past the few houses that separated me from theirs and up the driveway so I could hear clearly. I didn't want to mistake an owl or a cricket for a sex sound. Ducking in between Clifton's and Charles's cars, I listened with my hand across my mouth just in case I screamed. And sadly, my intuition had been dead on.

"I'm so sorry. Damn, I'm so sorry," I heard him apologizing to her in between pants.

Hearing Charles giving Mary the same stroke he'd given me while apologizing, I wanted to curl up on the pavement underneath one of their cars and wait to be run over. It felt like a fifty-ton weight had been dropped on top of my head and crushed me. I could barely stand on my own two feet to run to the car and get out of dodge. Charles had shown me who he was. *Now I must show him who I am.*

Chapter Twelve

Mary Bivens

In the shower, I washed all of Charles's scent off of me and replaced it with the Bath & Body Works shower gel that smelled like Mahogany's. Though I'd slept with Charles last night, I still woke up with the thoughts of a woman on my mind. Matter of fact, I'd dreamed of her last night and ended up waking up to check my phone to see she still hadn't accepted my request. I wanted to take the request back, but I was too scared to do so. I'd been in the shower for longer than usual trying to let the water soothe my nerves calm.

"Care for a shower buddy?"Charles pulled the shower curtain back, peeking in on me.

I jumped. "Oh, shit you scared me. I didn't hear you come in here."

Taking off his clothes and getting in, I guess he took me saying I had not heard him as, "Yes, jump on in," because he did.

"Turn around and let me wash you up," he said, grabbing the soap and the washcloth from my hand.

I was quiet as I turned around, wondering what all of this change of attitude business was about. It's like a light switch of affection had been flipped upward and on for me. He washed my back, my buttocks, underneath my arms, and even my toes before separating my legs to wash them and in between them. I grabbed a hold of the towel bar to keep my balance, damn near slipping and falling. I was turned on by the way he was touching me, but also because the scent of what I'd nicknamed Ms. Mahogany was floating around within the steam. I was riding a wave, getting pleased by my husband with the thought of how she'd pleased me on the massage table.

Charles leaned in for a kiss and trapped my tongue within his mouth. We hadn't kissed in so long, that the act on emotion seemed unreal. I didn't even know we could still connect as passionately as we were. Still, I thought about Mahogany while I was kissing him. I wondered what a kiss from her would feel like.

Grabbing my thigh, he lifted it up so I could feel the hardness of his cock as we kissed. The harder we kissed, the harder I felt him pressing into me. He didn't have an apology for me this morning. Or any words for that matter. All he had was an eager cock. That was good enough for me, though. My pussy was starting to flow faster than what the showerhead was squirting out. I couldn't help but grind on him and beg him to slide inside of me. The only thing I was feeling right now was the need to cum. So I did.

"I'll see you after work," he said, kissing my lips and leaving me in the shower to finish washing off.

I'd gotten into the shower confused and gotten out even more confused. The makeover that I'd gotten couldn't have been magical so I couldn't explain what was really up with Charles.

Getting dressed and grabbing a cup of coffee, I got ready to call Melissa back, but my phone alerted me with a notification that consumed all of me. It was Instagram alerting me that Mahogany had accepted me, requested me, and even sent me a private message that included her number.

Charles Bivens

After last night and this morning with Mary, I was driving to work with a new outlook on my marriage and trying to come up with a game plan for getting rid of Kandace. Even if I thought I was going to slip up in her from time to time after we'd gotten into it at her house, that was definitely out of the question now that I want to work it out with Mary. Kandace would be too much of a distraction.

Today's workload was intense. I had a million work tickets when I walked through the door, and even more calls. One of the departments rolled out a new database that required a lot of technical support. I didn't know how many times I repeated the same set of instructions, but I didn't complain. If technology were a simple thing to master, I wouldn't be able to set my salary or be in demand.

When my cell sounded off again, I thought it was another associate needing some support, but it was the college graduate girl, Tiffany. I'd forgotten all about her until I saw the name Thad pop up on my phone. I let my finger linger over the answer button, almost tapping it and saying hello. But I knew that one-word greeting and letting her know she had my attention would lead to something much more. I sent her to my voice-mail and proceeded to handle the woman I really needed to get straight, and gone.

"Kandace, can I see you in my office, please?" I called her into my office over the speaker phone.

"Yes, sir. I will be right in," she responded properly, enunciating each word perfectly. "How can I assist you?" she questioned once entering.

"What is with the voice change? Why are you talking like that?" I was not in the mood to play her games.

"I'm just keeping it professional and doing my job, sir."

"I'll have human resources delivering you a brown box if you keep antagonizing me," I threatened Kandace, ready to make the call.

"Do it. I dare you." She shrugged her shoulders. "Matter of fact, I'm begging you to. All you're going to do is end up looking like a fool and lose your job."

"Bitch, what?" I let my tongue slip.

She snickered. "Yeah, I'm going to let that slide because I would have been caught off guard too. But if you fire me, I will report you for inappropriate behavior and have you fired as well. I won't be the only one escorted out of here with a brown box in my hand."

"And what makes you think they would believe you? I'm established here, and you're just a low-level worker, from the temporary agency at that," I dissed her.

"Ha." She started cackling. "But just last month, I was 'an exemplary employee who should be hired in and given yet another raise.' Get the fuck out of here. If you try costing me my job, I'm going to ruin you too. Don't make me say that a third time."

I pushed the computer monitor I was working on to the floor out of anger, and it crashed and the screen shattered. "Damn." I was mad as hell but not about the monitor. My hands were tied when it came to firing Kandace, though that was the main thing I could hold over her head to keep her in line. She was absolutely right. I'd given her too many recommendations for awards, raises, and perks. I'd even put into writing that she should be hired into the company and placed into a salaried position. If I started badmouthing her now, I could be badmouthing myself indirectly as well.

It was starting to seem like the cake I had eaten was rotten, and the cake I was saving had spoiled. Our honeymoon period is officially over. Packing up my computer bag, I told my tech team I wasn't feeling well, and I jetted for the day. I needed a dose of China White to feel better.

Mary Bivens

"So, have you talked to your little girlfriend?" Jillian joked.

"Aw, hush with ya cougar ass," I got back with her.

"I'd rather be a cougar than a carpet muncher," she clowned me hard.

I started laughing and couldn't stop. "All right, girl. You got me. I can't believe you just said that."

"Me either. I am still shocked that your squeaky clean ass has vamped into a bad girl. You finally have some dirt I can dish when you piss me off."

Whenever me and Jillian talked, there were a few minutes dedicated just to joking on one another. It was all fun and games, though. I'd never been offended, and I was not about to get in my feelings today.

"Anyway, back to your question: yes, I have talked to her. We have been talking and text messaging since you told me to send her a friend request," I happily admitted.

"What? Have you? Oh my God," she shouted loud enough for my neighbors to hear her out in California.

"It has been crazy, Jillie. I have been sending her naked pictures of me, video chatting with her, and even looking up lesbian pornos to see if I can really handle a bisexual experience. We have been talking all day. I mean, it's been like ten hours."

"Say what now? Whoa, let me drink some water and catch my breath because I wasn't expecting you to drop that bomb. I didn't know you were that serious." She drew out the word "that." "I was just playing when I called you a carpet muncher earlier but are you ready for that for real? You know that's like part of the criteria of being bisexual."

I sighed. "Yeah, I know and that's part of what I'm nervous about. That and getting fucked by her with a strap-on."

"Whoa," she said again. "You keep dropping bombs on me, Mary. I'm not used to you talking like this."

"Well, hurry up and get used to it so you can give me some more advice. She invited me over to her house later on." I really wanted to know what Jillian thought.

"You already know what I think, sis. I told you yesterday. If I were you, I would've been gone and getting some the whole day Charles was at work."

I was hesitant to say yes to Mahogany at first. I knew I'd been flirting and leading her on with innuendos about taking it to the next level, so I knew I could be stepping into slippery territory, literally. But I followed Jillian's advice and asked for the address.

Chapter Thirteen

Mary Bivens

My hands were trembling as they gripped the wheel. I almost came up off the freeway twice to turn around and go home. I was nervous about being alone with Mahogany again. I knew the sexual tension between us would be thick, especially since it had gotten so heavy in the massage room. She had just about done everything to me besides fuck me. Plus, we'd been sending text messages to one another that were extremely suggestive that I would take it there. Though I wasn't sure I was ready to make good on my words, I chose to keep going because I wanted to see where the road ahead was going to lead to.

"Hey, beautiful. I am so glad you did not flake out on me," she greeted me, then held her hand out to help guide me into the door.

It felt like butterflies were swarming around in my stomach as I stepped inside and looked around at her quaint and cute spot. I was sure my face was flushed from blushing. I was shaking in my tennis shoes.

Picking up on my nervousness, Mahogany starting making light conversation with me that could break the ice. After she showed me the few hundred feet of her apartment and what she'd cooked for us to dine on, I couldn't keep my mouth closed. I tasted from every pot and pan but dessert. The ice was broken because we both knew how to cook and had a love for food.

Dinner was delicious. Mahogany had the table set up nicely, and each of the portions she'd prepared were perfect and left me wanting a little bit more. In my mind, I was thinking that it would be cool to cook with her one day. But my lips did not part to speak those thoughts.

"Everything is so good, Mahogany. Thank you for cooking for me."

"It was my pleasure. I know how to heat up things in more rooms than just the bedroom."

"And the massage room," I tried opening up, sliding a little humor in from my end.

We both laughed, but I started slipping back into a shell. I knew that once I stepped outside of my boundaries, I couldn't go back. I was trying to get my courage up enough to even have some courage. I was taking it one second at a time.

I kept stuffing my mouth with food so I wouldn't have to say much during the conversation. I didn't want to say too much, and I didn't want to say the wrong thing, either. I hadn't dated any other women to know how to date Mahogany. I thought she could tell I was a little out of my element and uncomfortable because she didn't force any subjects on me, but rather kept the conversation simple and light. We talked about stuff that was happening in the news, what our hobbies were, and of course what made me so tense on her massage table. Of course I knew that question would come up. It was what initially brought us together. By the time she'd asked, though, I had enough wine in my system to speak freely.

The love/hate story of Charles and me didn't get any better, nor did it change. Even though I was giving her the short version, I still ended up crying. I could be strong about the subject one minute and extremely weak about it the very next.

Pushing her seat back from the table, she got up and pulled my seat back some, and then held her hands out for me to grab them and stand up. I couldn't call her a gentleman because she was not a man, but she was loving and nurturing to all of my needs. I was appreciative. When I got to my feet, she hugged me tightly. Kind of how Jillian used to do when she was consoling me, but a lot more intimate and sexual. The longer she held me, the weaker I felt. I ended up shifting all of my weight on her.

"It is okay to break down, Mary. I am right here to make you feel better and help you get back up," she consoled me.

I was not sure if I believed her or if at the moment she said the exact words that I needed to hear, but I found solace within them. It felt good being able to break down with someone and then get a hug afterward. I was not taking anything away from Jillian, because without her, I would not be right here right now with Mahogany, but it felt both good and empowering to be held in a supporter's arms.

Mahogany and I went to the couch to watch television. It almost did not seem like I was chilling with a female I had been having sexual feelings and fantasies about, until she picked my foot up in her hand and started rubbing it. Moans started slipping from my mouth. Just like on her massage table, I couldn't control myself.

She moved her hand up and down my foot, ankle, and then the calf muscle of my leg. I was holding on to the couch cushion for dear life. When she started on the second foot, I ended up clenching my booty muscles together to fight against the wave that was rushing through my body. For all the stress that Charles put into my body over the last few days, she was making it melt away.

As soft as Mahogany's hands were, they were slick. Before I knew it, they were up my leg and on my thighs, working the meat of them in circles. I felt my panties getting wet. I shocked myself when I didn't move her hands or myself. In fact, I slid my ass down farther on the couch so she could have easier access to the prize between my legs. I wanted her to hurry up and take me before I lost all of my confidence and courage. Biting my lip, squeezing my eyes together, and shaking all over, I was lost in Mahogany's trance until she stopped.

"I don't want our first time to be on this couch or on the floor. Can I take you to my bed?"

Never ever had I been asked that question by a woman before and never ever would I have said yes, until tonight.

Getting up, Mahogany picked an album on her iPhone and then placed it on the dock. The music blasted through the speakers and filled the room. It sounded like I was in attendance of a live jazz concert. Walking over to me, she took my hand and led me down the small hallway to her bedroom. She didn't have to drag me. I took each step with confidence and surety that I'd be able to go through what I knew was next. Chill time was over. I knew shit was about to turn up and get hot.

Once we got into her bedroom, she put on a small dance show for me, undressing herself to the beat. Her mocha-colored skin looked flawless under the recessed lights and against the flickering candles. I didn't feel strange looking at her full breasts, her darkened, hard nipples, or the bare skin that surrounded her prized possession. I'd watched enough lesbian pornos to feel comfortable.

"Can I take off your clothes?" She danced up to me, kissing me on the sly.

I nodded that she could, not afraid that my voice would crack, but that she would slip her tongue inside of my mouth. I was all for being touched, kissed, and fondled, but I was still worried about whether I'd be able to perform with and for a woman.

I was absolutely quiet as she took off my pants and shirt but then had me melting when she acknowledged my undergarments.

"Very pretty panty and bra set. Sexy," she purred, kissing on my belly button.

No words were needed for that part. It wasn't until she started softly kissing all of my other body parts did I start losing my balance and momentum.

"Breathe." She felt me tensing up. "The best experience is yet to come. Lie down on your stomach just like you would do if you were at the spa."

She didn't have to tell me twice. Lying down on her bed, I smelled her sweet perfume within the blanket and then rested my head on one of the pillows. I taking deep breaths not only to slow my heart down but to inhale her scent so I could get my own bottle of the perfume. I was too embarrassed to ask for the name of the fragrance that was so intoxicating.

I heard Mahogany fumbling around in the nightstand drawer that was beside the bed, but I didn't open my eyes up to see what she was looking for. I didn't want to ruin the surprise. Instead, I tried zoning out to the music that was playing through the speakers.

She straddled my back. I felt she was just as warm and wet as I was. It felt like a pitcher of warm tea had been poured onto my back. Knowing that my body was bringing her pleasure made my pussy lips start to moisten. She started kissing from the center of my neck and then down my back to the arch of it. My clit was jumping, tapping against the sheet each time it pulsated from her caress.

"Just the same as I told you when you got a massage that day, relax and take some deep breaths." Her voice was almost lost within the music.

Then I felt what she must have been fumbling in the
nightstand drawer for: some warm massage oil that
made my skin feel even hotter. Mahogany was good at
what she did for sure. She rubbed away all of my nervousness with one swoop, then traced the outside of my lips
with her fingers before slipping two of them inside of my
tunnel.

"Oh, shit. Don't stop," slipped from my mouth, mixed
with drool and moans.

Though I was fighting hard against acting like a virgin,
I couldn't stop moaning, gripping the blanket, or screaming into the pillow. I was all over her bed. Fingering me
softly and then quickly, she kept tapping on my G-spot
and breaking me in. If and when I watch lesbian pornos
again, I'll be able to compare their freak show with what
I was going through.

"Flip over." She took charge even more.

I did, and found myself screaming to the ceiling.
Charles and the entire twenty years I invested into him
and our family became a distant memory as she loved all
over me. Mahogany wasn't missing an inch of my skin as
her tongue licked my nipples, her teeth pulled at my nipples, and then her tongue continued exploring my body.
Up and down my arms, my legs, and the spine of my back,
she rubbed my body to the beat of the music like she was
a musician.

"All of this feels so good, so right. Oh my God," I spoke
my thoughts out loud, throwing my hands behind my
head and clutching the pillow.

Stopping her massage, Mahogany gripped my wrists
and held them behind my head. Kissing me from my belly button to my lips, she then climbed on top of me and
rubbed her pussy over mine. The feeling of bare skin on
bare skin felt surprisingly different. Her clit jumping
on mine felt even better than that. "You are about to get
your mind blown," she hissed sexily.

Before I could blink, she was off of me and spreading my legs. I gasped when her tongue tickled my clitoris. And I cried when she spread my lips and ate me out. She was better at it than Charles had ever been. I locked my thighs around her head. She didn't seem to care how rough I pushing my pelvis into her face. I couldn't help myself. The more I pushed myself into her, the more she hummed and tugged at my clit. I was screaming for mercy, but she wasn't letting up. It felt like I was having an out-of-body experience. She was a savage and I was her prey.

Mahogany

Mary was about to pass out from the sex I was putting down on her. I was enjoying every minute of controlling her body. Biting her bottom lip, she damn near swallowed it when I started flicking her clit with my tongue and fingering her at the same time. Each time I plunged into her juiciness, and she squirmed, my kitty cat got wetter. I didn't know if she knew she was going to eat some pussy for the first time, but she was. I'd tell her how to do it step by step if she needed me to.

"Are you gonna let me have this pussy all to myself soon?" I took a breath from going down on her, wanting her to feed my ego.

"Yes. Yes, I promise," she shouted.

I hoped her words weren't empty of emotion. I was becoming needy and possessive for this woman. "When?" I pressed the point.

"Soon. I promise. I need you, baby," she moaned, lifting her hips up. She was desperate for my tongue game.

Switching my sex style up, I started rubbing my finger across her wet clit and up and down her slit slowly and then real fast. The trick was to keep switching it up so she wouldn't know which one was coming next. She was begging me not to stop. Her mouth was begging me to make her feel good. And her body was reacting to every touch I placed on her body like she hadn't been pleased in years. She had the most peaceful and serene look on her face as she lay in my bed with her eyes tightly closed.

"This feels so damn good." Her voice was low but still audible.

"I know it does. Make sure you're paying attention to how it's done so you can return the favor when it's your turn." I took the opportunity to warn her of what was coming so she could mentally prepare herself.

"Huh?" Her body tensed up just as I'd expected it to. "I've never done any of this to a woman. You're my first experience." She told me something I already knew.

"Don't worry, I'll teach you. And something tells me you're a fast learner. All you have to do is everything I have done and am about to do to you."

Taking a deep breath, she agreed to my terms like she had a choice not to agree with them. I was not the type of woman who didn't get or take what I wanted. Women were included within that bunch.

Pinching her nipples, I got them as erect as they could get before kissing and pulling on them with my teeth. "Are you ready for me to give you something hard between your legs?" I was ready to turn her all the way out.

From her quivering, I knew she was scared to respond with the answer yes, but she did.

Going into my bedside drawer, I pulled out a couple of dildos: a small one to get her started off with and a medium-sized one to make her head spin. I wanted Mary to see stars within my bed with me between her legs. I wanted to sexually please her better than her husband had in twenty years. I wanted her to make good on her word and leave his ass. I needed to take advantage of this moment. This was my chance to turn Mary out.

Mary's eyes said she was nervous, but she did not stop me from pushing her legs apart.

"Don't be scared. I got you. And I am about to make you feel better than your husband has ever made you feel." My confidence grew with each word. I was about to go into a competition with a man who could lay the pipe better and win. There was not a rule that read a pipe must be of flesh.

"I trust you, Mahogany. I am ready for this." She pulled me down into a kiss, caressing my buttocks and running her fingers up and down my spine.

Her heart felt like it was getting ready to jump into my chest from the intensity of the beats. She couldn't let go of me, and I refused to get off of her. It felt like our bodies were melting into one another's, with the boiling points being our pussies.

Taking the rabbit sex toy, I turned the vibration speed up and placed the cold ball on her bulge. She jumped from the sudden temperature change but adjusted quickly because of the sensations the toy was sending through her body. I knew she was ready to cum. I could tell from how her body squirmed and how quickly her lips sucked the bullet up.

"I guess you have been watching those pornos," I teased.

She blushed, then quivered even harder than she had been because I'd strategically turned the vibration speed up. Once she thought she'd gotten my strategies all figured out, I placed the rabbit ears on her bulge and let it do its job on a low vibration speed. Her knees kept knocking, and she kept pushing her booty down, trying to feel more of the vibration. I was intentionally teasing her, making her desperate to cum. The longer it built up, the better the explosion would be. I not only want to physically fuck her but emotionally as well.

Licking down her neck to her chest, I took both of her breasts into my mouth and started suckling like a newborn. Her skin was so smooth and tasted sweet like strawberries, especially around her nipples. I knew from experience that the flavor was from an edible collection.

The best thing about dildos was that you could buy the exact size and style you wanted. They came fresh out of the box like the real thing, veins and all, without all of the bullshit cheating that men came with. Nowadays, they even had vaginas that were so similar to a woman's that it was scary. It did everything but get wet and cum, but there was jelly and lubricant for that. For this vibrating dildo I was about to give it to Mary with, it was five inches in size and controlled by me. I was about to fuck her with my strap-on.

Placing the tip of it to the opening of her wet vagina, I didn't have time to tease her again because she spread her legs and pulled me in.

"Oh, yeah? Are you sure you want it rough like that?"

"Yes, just like that. Please," she begged, pointing her toes to the ceiling and spreading her legs wider so the dildo could go deeper.

I took the cue and started killing her with my strokes. Each time she threw her hips up, I plunged into her wetness like a ferocious lion. I got off being at an absolute point of power, having her submissively laid out underneath me. I started working the strap-on like I was born with it. I was giving her body the business with one deep stroke after the next. At first she kept trying to keep up by thrusting her pussy into me, but I damn near made her pass out when I turned the vibration up as far as it would go while it was inside of her. Even with all the squealing my girlfriend, Jasmine, did, I was sure none of my neighbors had heard a woman scream through their walls as loudly as Mary.

"I bet your husband's dick can't spin and make you scream like that," I boasted, acting like the piece of plastic was truly attached to me by skin.

She shook her head no.

"So, do you wanna see what it feels like to ride it?"

"I don't know," she stuttered, starting to seem self-conscious.

After a little more coaxing from me, Mary finally gave in and made the five-inch strap on disappear up inside of her pussy. I could feel her warmth and wetness on my thighs, sliding down onto my own hotbox. I couldn't wait to fill her up with a larger one later on, since she'd mastered this one. My main plan was to get Mary to let go of all her inhibitions and insecurities. I had a lot of work to do, and I was going to enjoy putting in the hours.

Chapter Fourteen

Mary Bivens

"Babe, I've got an early meeting, so I've gotta get out here to beat the traffic. I'll call you in a couple of hours." Charles woke me up with his plans, then kissed me on the mouth with my morning breath and all.

"Okay. Have a good day." I fell back onto my pillow, not recognizing the man walking out of the bedroom door.

"You too. Love you, and I'll see you tonight," he said; then the door slammed.

My husband hadn't been the same since the night he randomly crept into our room to make love. I felt like he and I were going through the honeymoon period of our relationship again. The feeling of being a happy wife had become a rarity, so I was clutching on to it for dear life. I didn't want this happy phase we were experiencing to end.

Not only had Charles come home early every night, but we had been having sex like teenagers, too. On the same site I found the lesbian porn, I did some research on how to pleasure Charles. Who says you can't teach an old dog new tricks? Mahogany had done more than add a little spice to our sex life, putting a little fire up under my ass to add more flavor and variety with stunts and props.

I'd turned it all the way up in the bedroom with Charles. Well, more like all over the house. I was doing unpredictable stuff like meeting him nude at the door, creeping into his man cave dressed up like sexy characters, and even trying new sex toys, seeming like a professional. The Internet has been my best source of knowledge. There wasn't a thing you couldn't search for on Google.

Getting ready to curl back up with my pillow, my phone started vibrating across the nightstand. I grabbed it just before it hit the floor, but I didn't answer it. It was Mahogany texting me that she had something special planned for us tonight. I had been nothing but naughty with Mahogany and I couldn't wait to see what was in store for tonight.

It had been about a week, and I had been living a double life with her and my husband. Realistically, Mahogany was getting more of my time than Charles and tonight's time hadn't even been added to the tally. What I was doing was fun. She brought out the good and the bad in me at the same time.

"Have you ever cum while listening to spoken word?" she asked while keeping her eyes on the road.

"I have never been to spoken word," I honestly revealed, feeling as if I was out of touch with the times.

"Hmmm, well, I'm glad I can be the first." She smiled while pulling up inside of what seemed like a full parking lot.

"So we're going to one of those spoken jams, huh?" I eagerly asked. I was sure she could hear the hint of excitement in my voice.

"Maybe. Yes." She giggled as I hopped up and down in my seat as if I were some sort of small child opening up an early Christmas present.

Once she parked, I unlocked my seat belt and opened the door myself.

"Hmm, I hope you're excited to cum, not hear the poems."

That statement stopped me dead in my tracks for a moment, before I fired back and said, "If you can make me cum, that is." I heard her suck in her teeth and I couldn't help but laugh.

"Oh, you know I can." She slid out, and together we closed the doors before she locked them. And, just like that, hand in hand, we headed toward the front entrance of the building. The doors were opened by a nicely built female, but my eyes weren't on her. Mahogany had my undivided attention whether she wanted it or not. But I had a feeling that she did.

Once inside, I soon discovered that the woman who had my nose so far open a car could fit in it was a regular. She reached backward for my hand. I felt her soft yet strong grip. She led us over to an empty table then pulled a lighter out of her bag to light the red globed candle.

I roamed a little with my eyes and noticed that the place had a lovely setting. Nothing fancy, yet nothing that looked like it belonged in the back with the trash, either. I also noticed the place was filed with females only.

Mahogany placed her hands over mine and gave me that devious smirk that always sent chills down my spine: that "I could eat you alive" stare that my body used to ache for Charles to give me.

"Is this a lesbian spoken word night?" I asked under my breath, hoping not to offend anyone.

"Every day is lesbian day here, baby doll." With a huge smile, she removed her hand from mine, then seductively placed it on my upper thigh. I felt a sudden shockwave shoot through my entire body. Once again this woman had me blushing as if I were some sort of schoolgirl out on her first date.

"Okay now, be good." I playfully brushed her hand away knowing my cat was going to be getting moist at any moment.

Mahogany laughed at me knowing full well the effect she had on me. She knew I was gone off her touch; even a blind man could see that. "Yeah, baby doll, I'll be good until the lights go off."

On cue, as if the freak goddess heard her, the light went dim. Back on her mission, her hands moved right back to my thighs. This time she applied more pressure to her slow strokes. I let out a giggle while others started to snap their fingers. One by one magic was spoken from the mic; and, when Mahogany was called to the stage, I felt my heart speed up.

"Baby doll," she breathed into the mic, keeping her eyes focused on me and only me. I felt as if she were taking my breath away. My mouth felt dry as if I could not speak, or even swallow for that matter. She was captivating. It was as if we were inside of the crowded cafe all alone, just me and her. My new beloved told me she would have my panties wet and that was an understatement. My shit was soaked when she got done speaking, and it pained me to wonder if any other females' panties were soaking like mine from her deep words of love, lust, and devotion. Everyone snapped their fingers and hollered as she stepped down and made it back to me.

"How wet are you now?" this fabulous woman I craved licked my earlobe while asking.

"Place that hand below and see." I was not sure what got over me, but I did know I was not ending this night without her making me cum.

Like a vampire on a diet she lightly bit my neck while moving her hands between my thighs. Before she could go any further, the lights went from dim to bright. Mahogany stood, helped me up, and grabbed our coats from behind the seats. She helped me into mine before getting into her own. I swear she was doing all the things Charles used to do and making me feel like he used to do.

"Let's go, baby doll," was softly demanded of me.

I didn't reject. I didn't talk back. I wasted no time to comply as I reached for my purse. I wanted to get the hell out the moment she said the word "baby."

As we made our way for the door, people tried to speak, but she just did a few waves and yelled "I'll call you later" a few times before we finally felt the wind on our faces. Going to the car, she unlocked the door and helped me inside, before rushing to the driver's side. Once in, she slammed the door, and her lips found mine in a heavy yet passionate kiss. Once the kiss broke, our breathing was like we just finished running a marathon. I could not help myself as I blushed once more.

"You're so fucking sexy when you blush." My girl moved a string of my hair that was dangling in front of my face. I was caught in my feelings as if this were some corny love story I had read late one night alone in bed, pining away over my AWOL husband.

"Thank you." I tried to cover my face because I knew I was about to blush again, but she placed her hands over mine.

"You ready?" she asked.

"Yes."

She kissed me for a short amount of time before starting the car up again. When she finally stopped the car, we were somewhere on a moderate hill. She unbuckled her seat belt, turned to me, and caressed my face with her fingers.

"Have you ever made love in the back seat of a car?" she asked, bringing her thumb to my mouth. I gladly opened up and sucked on it like a lollipop before bringing it out of my mouth. I moaned from how wet that minor yet exciting moment had me feeling.

"No," I answered with all honesty.

"Want to give it a go?" Her thumb was tracing the out-
line of my lips.

"Yes," I breathed out.

She unbuckled my seat belt, and together we opened
the car door and stepped out. The cold air hit me, but the
hot feeling Mahogany had me feeling quickly replaced
the coldness. She came to me, hands back caressing my
face, before opening the back door, and leading me inside first. I paused, taking our coats off and then throwing them in the front seat, before grabbing the back of her
head, and bringing it down for a sloppy kiss. She moaned
in my mouth. I moaned in hers.

Could this car rock? I'd soon find that out tonight.

"Hey, I made it home," I slurred into the phone.

"I wish you would've spent the night."

"I wish I could have too. I swear it won't be long before I leave Charles and can cuddle up to you all night
long," I lied, hoping that I was buying myself more time
to play around with her.

Though I had feelings for Mahogany, they don't equate
to "divorce Charles at the end of the day." I wasn't even
sure if I was a bisexual, or just curious and acting out as
a bored and cheated-on housewife. The most important
thing for me right now was to cater to me. And if that
meant playing both Charles and Mahogany to get my
needs satisfied, then so be it.

"Why don't you turn around and leave that lame-ass
nigga tonight, Mary?" Mahogany was persistent.

Pushing out a deep breath of air, I then took a big gulp
of water. I'd been sipping from the bottle since I left
Mahogany's house in an effort to sober up some. "Why
don't I just call you in the morning?"

"Better yet, why don't you text me while you're lying
next to him? I'll be waiting." She hung up.

"You sure will be," I said out loud, powering my phone off.

Though I could play those games with her when Charles was creeping into the house with a different ho's perfume on every day and night, I couldn't now that he was cuddling up to me.

Charles, from what I could tell, was putting all of his effort into me. He'd been home every night for dinner, romantic every morning, and even attentive during the day with text messages. I hadn't even been able to sneak around with Mahogany like we had when we first started up our love thang because Charles checked in more. It was becoming too hard to juggle the both of them and their needs, though they both perfectly met my needs. It hurt me to know Charles probably felt that way about me and a few other women at some point in time of him cheating, which was why I couldn't stop reaching back out to Mahogany. He'd created a reason for her.

Walking into the foyer, I hung up my coat and dropped my bag, ready to walk up the stairs and crawl into bed.

"Hey, Ma. You're in trouble," Clifton said.

"Why and what do you mean?" My heart started fluttering, worried that I'd been found out. Someone definitely could have seen me with Mahogany and snitched on me by now.

"Because Dad had a whole romantic night set up for you two and you're just now coming home."

"Oh, no. He did? Wow. I thought he was working late."

"That was just the play-off so he could surprise you. He went up to y'all bedroom about an hour ago with a bottle of Hennessy."

Shit, I thought, knowing I'd have to come up with a good excuse. "Thanks, son, and I will see you in the morning. Let me get upstairs and smooth things over with your father."

"Okay, Ma. Good night and good luck. Oh, and if I were you, I'd wash off that stinking perfume you have on."

"Thanks," I said over my shoulder, hurrying to the powder room we had on the first floor so I could wash off the lingering scent of Mahogany's perfume.

Instead of me feeling justified for cheating since I'd been cheated on, I felt bad for treating Charles exactly how I hated to be treated. I felt like a hypocrite.

Our room was dark except for the flicker coming from the television. It was of course tuned into a sports channel. Charles lay on the bed with a bottle of Hennessy beside him on the nightstand. It looked like there were only a few drops left and I didn't see a juice bottle, which meant his ass had been guzzling and was lit. I almost didn't want to wake him up because I didn't know if he was going to be upset. Charles had a tendency of snapping recklessly, especially once he'd gotten some liquor in his system.

I loosened up his pants real fast and started kissing on his dick. I even slurped it all in my mouth a few times before it was all the way stiffened up.

Waking up, he looked at me through the slits of his half-closed eyes and grabbed the back of my head to push it down farther. I swallowed as much of his dick as I could without gagging. All that watching porno made me a pro.

Reaching down and in between my legs, he started stroking my clitoris so I could cum at the same time as him. That turned me on even more. I was keeping his testicles warm with both my hands and my spit, switching between them and his manhood with my mouth. The new tricks I was putting on him were making his body quiver underneath me. He barely could flick my clitoris the right way. I kept having to push myself down on his finger to get some stimulation.

Not wanting him to bust one and leave me filled up, I released the jaw lock I had on him and sat up to straddle him instead. I sat all the way down on his length; then he held me by the waist and pushed himself as far inside of me as he could go. Within two seconds, he let off an explosion inside of me and pushed me off to the side of him and fluffed his pillow.

"We will talk about where you were at tomorrow."

Chapter Fifteen

Mary Bivens

Rolling my eyes, I was irritated that Charles wouldn't get off my heels or give me a second to breathe alone. I didn't care about him being nervous about me cheating. I was trying to video chat with Mahogany. A couple of weeks ago, he barely knew I existed. Now he acted like he couldn't live without me. I was almost tempted to start an argument so he would retire either to the man cave or to the house of whatever bitch had been keeping his attention all this damn time. I really didn't care.

"Where have you been at all day? I got off early to take you on a surprise lunch, but you weren't here. You keep not being here when I come home to surprise you."

"I know."

"Okay. So back to my original question. Where were you? I got here at noon, and it is now after eight at night." He wasn't playing the position he'd given me to play for years very well at all.

I ignored him and began undressing for a shower, hoping that he'd get the point and push on.

"Mary, what is wrong with you? Don't you hear me talking?"He was getting louder and louder.

"Yeah, I hear you talking, Charles," I responded nonchalantly. "But I just don't care to answer you. You know how it is." I took two steps toward the bathroom. I was pulled back four steps by my arm.

"And what in the hell is that supposed to mean?"

"Let go of my arm, Charles," I calmly spoke. When he didn't move to let me go fast enough, I started snatching my arm back from his grip. "Just like I couldn't hold on to you when you didn't want to be kept, you can't hold on to me."

"You're doing a whole lot of talking to not be saying anything, Mary. Are you fucking around with another man? Huh? Do you have some nigga stashed somewhere who's been giving you dick during the day?" Charles had the nerve to look like he was hurt by the thought of me stepping out on him. I was offended.

"And what if I do?" I tested the waters.

He dropped my arm. "Then you better call that mutha-fucka and tell him it's over. I love my wife, and I want my wife."

I giggled then rolled my eyes. "For real, Charles? What electrician helped you turn that light bulb on?"

"Where is all this attitude coming from? Call that nigga right now," he demanded, starting to move toward my phone. My heart sank. If Charles went through my phone, he was going to find a gang of inappropriate pictures, text messages, and conversation logs from me and Mahogany.

"Quit tripping, Charles. Damn. You know good and damn well that I'm not cheating on you. There is not another man," I specifically said "man" on purpose, only halfway lying. "I just wanted you to know how it felt to not know where I was at for a change. I am always here when you come home, answering the phone when you call, and jumping when you say get something done. I saw you were home when I was coming home earlier, and I decided to keep driving. I took myself to that new Tyler Perry movie."

No part of me felt bad for lying because I was also laying the truth on him. I did want him to know how it felt. Had my phone not been unlocked and accessible, I would have kept my act going. It was a good feeling to see Charles sweating over me for a change.

"I deserve that." He bowed down. "Look, I know there is not a way possible to erase the past, but I am really trying to prove myself to you now. As fucked up as this might sound, all that messing around I did only made me realize I had something much more priceless at home."

"Unfortunately for you, that is not making me feel any better. Not one fucking bit. If it took for you to cheat on me, bring me home a sexually transmitted disease that ended up making me miscarry, and taunting me with divorce papers for damn near four years, then you really don't love me and are settling just because you're getting old and the game is played out. Excuse me."

Moving past him, I felt the waterfall of tears building up, and I wanted to be out of his face before they fell. He grabbed my arm again. This time when I turned around, he was on his knees with tears streaming down his face. Seeing him like that tugged at my heart. For the first time in a very long time, we were on the same emotional level: pain. There was a sadness in his eyes that I could relate to.

"Mary, sweetheart," he said, choking up, "I don't want to say the wrong thing trying to say the right thing. I don't want to make things worse than I already have, because I can't lose you. I don't want to lose you. Even if it means spending the rest of my days making it up to you, I am willing to do that. Please tell me that you will try." His voice cracked through every word of his supposed confessional.

Turning away, I was not ready to face him and forgive him. I had spent so much energy and time getting through the horrible pain he continuously put me through that I did not want to go backward now that I was finally starting to feel free. I didn't want to feel the same pain again.

"Mary, please look at me. Please," he was begging. "If you tell me what you want, I'll get it. I'll do it."

"Where is all this coming from?" I stuttered. "Why now? Why should I believe you love me now?" It was the realest question I could ask.

Letting one of my arms go, he pulled his cell phone from his pocket and told Siri to call his attorney. I already knew what he was going to say, but I chose to let everything play out.

The attorney answered after three rings. "Charles, good evening."

"Hey, Paul, do me a favor first thing in the morning and put a stop to any- and everything regarding my divorce. Instead of clocking me for those hours, bill me for drawing up an account for Mary only, which has twenty thousand in it, and then put her name on my private account with the same privileges I have."

"But, sir—" It was clear the attorney was about to contest.

"No advisement is needed, Paul. Let me know once you have finished setting everything up, and I will stop by the office to pick up the paperwork. Are we good?"

"We are good," the attorney responded to Charles as dryly as he could. "I will speak with you tomorrow. Have a good night."

I lost my breath during the conversation, totally not expecting him to tell the attorney what he had. It was one thing for him to call the divorce off. But it was a major thing for him to give me my own personal account with twenty racks in it and access to his business account. I would be set up swell after tomorrow, and I could wipe his ass right out of everything as payback. Charles couldn't survive without his money. I knew what he was doing. He didn't even have to say it.

"What else can I do to show you that I am very serious about you and me?" He was groveling. "What can I do to prove myself to you?"

Looking down at my husband, I couldn't help but pull him up. I felt stupid for having a feeling other than hatred toward him, but I also wanted to see what life with a better version of him would be like. It's kinda like running a marathon and quitting right before the final lap. If there'd be a trophy at the end of my race with Charles, I wanted it. Especially because what me and Mahogany had was only for fun.

"There can't be another woman, another slip-up, another apology, Charles. From here on out, everything must be official with you or it's going to be over for real. I'm willing to try but not like how you are used to me trying. I cannot and will not be hurt again." I felt strong speaking, finally. Mahogany was a fix in more than one way.

"I just gave you my lifeline, Mary. I will now spend however long it takes to show you that you also have my heart."

Chapter Sixteen

Mary Bivens

Dressed completely down in pajamas, a head scarf, and mismatched socks, I moved around the kitchen preparing dinner. On the menu was baked chicken, macaroni and cheese, cornbread dressing from scratch, and a batch of fresh vegetables that I'd chopped, seasoned, and steamed. I couldn't wait to pile me a plate up and plop down in front of the television. Charles said he would be home by dinnertime, but I was not going to be shocked if he failed to make good on his words.

Hearing my phone ring, I dried my hands and went to look at it. It was Mahogany calling me over and over again, but I'd been ignoring each one of the calls. It wasn't that I didn't want to see her again. That was the exact opposite of my intentions. It was just the wrong time. Charles and I were finally happy, and I didn't want that bubble popped.

She called back to back before leaving a voice-mail. I deleted it just as the same I'd done them all. I'd been blocking all of her text messages from coming through, too.

"Mary, where are you?" I heard Charles scream into the house as if he were crazy.

"Yeah. I'm in the kitchen. Here I come." I hurried up and powered my phone off while walking to meet him in the foyer. I hadn't heard him pull into the driveway, nor had I expected him home. It was only six in the evening. The only thing that crossed my mind was that something was wrong. "Is everything okay?" I asked with a stuttering voice.

"Hey, baby." He leaned in and kissed me on the forehead. "Nope, everything hasn't been okay, but I'm about to make it that way."

"Huh? What? Stop talking in circles and tell me what's going on. Is something wrong with Melissa or Clifton?" I didn't understand what Charles's answer meant, and I wasn't in the mood for the word games he liked to play at his leisure.

"No, nothing is wrong with the kids, Mary. I just got off the phone with Clifton, and he is staying at the dorm with Melissa tonight."

"Oh, okay." I sighed, assuming he still hadn't spoken to Melissa. "Then what are you talking about? What's not all right?"

"Oh my God, woman; us. We haven't been right." He sounded like he'd just tripped upon a new revelation that had been brewing for years.

"Nope, not in a very long time," I agreed with him, though I wasn't sure where the conversation was about to end up.

"Right but, tonight, I want to take another step toward showing you how committed I am to making this marriage work. My company is having a party tonight and I want you there with me on my arm."

I was speechless. Charles had not asked me to go on a date with him or be around him and his associates in months. And, before then, he had put a stop to me popping up with picnic baskets for lunch. As funny as he was acting the last time I called myself surprising him with a romantic lunch, I wondered if he still even wore his wedding ring at work.

"Mary? Did you hear me?" he asked, waving his hand in front of my face.

I was certain there was a glassy glaze over my eyes. "Yeah, I heard you. I'll be ready in a few."

Skipping up the stairs two at a time, I was about to beat my face with makeup to perfection, fix my hair up cutely, and get dressed in record time. I could not wait to go on a date with Charles. This new him, which reminded me of the old him, had my heart fluttering and my belly feeling like butterflies were swarming around in it. I never stopped loving my husband. I just hated all of the cruel things he'd done to me.

It was easy to find a sexy outfit to wear since I had a brand new wardrobe of stylish clothes. I was about to wow him and all of his coworkers with my new flair. The last time I went on Charles's arm to work event, I was in a drab gown with pearls on. Besides that, they were used to seeing me in khaki pants and floral print shirts with pendants clipped to them. I was planning on dropping jaws at tonight's function.

Sliding on a slinky black body-con dress with a pair of black Christian Louboutin heels, I accessorized the outfit with gold bangles and a pair of yellow diamond earrings. I didn't need a necklace because it would have been too gaudy, and I opted to carry a wristlet instead of a purse because I didn't want anything to clash with the oval-shaped cut and dip that made my dress to die for. Jillian would have been proud. Mahogany would have been too, but I was trying extremely hard to block her out of my mental.

Charles must have heard my heels coming down the staircase because, once I hit the last step, he met me in the foyer with a glass of wine for me in his hand. "Damn, you look absolutely breathtaking." He raised my arm so I could twirl around in a circle. "I am the luckiest man on earth."

Hearing Charles compliment me made me feel sexier than I had when I looked in the mirror upstairs when I slipped on a black lace thong. Though I was trying to push Mahogany out of my mental, she'd given me the confidence that was shining through tonight. Damn, I missed her; but I didn't have time to think about her. My life had to go on and, right now, it was moving along smoothly with my husband. Charles was looking at me with drool coming from the sides of his mouth.

"Thank you, baby. Since you're putting forth a great effort to show me that you are still one hundred percent devoted to me and this marriage, the least I could do was step it up a few notches and show you that I am worth it."

"Naw, Mary. You have been worth it. It is I who needs to expend as much energy as possible proving my worthiness of your love."

As of late, Charles couldn't seem to say the wrong thing. I kept waiting for him to slip back into his old ways but he had been moving carefully and lovingly. I was not used to this new and improved Charles, but it was refreshing to feel appreciated. If only I could have him and Mahogany at the same time, things would have been perfect.

"Are you ready, my dear?" He bowed and kissed my hand.

"Yes, I am." I blushed. *Yeah, a girl can get used to this.*

"Then, let's go before these drunks drink the bar out of liquor." He held the door open just as he used to do. I giggled and walked through it and ended up laughing even more at Charles being flirtatious and silly. "Yeah, let's hurry up and get there so I can get some drinks up in you. That booty is looking mighty right."

It took us twenty minutes to arrive at the restaurant. Waiting for the valet attendant to finish up with the car ahead of us, I flipped the sun visor down to check my makeup one last time. I wanted to look flawless just in case we ran into a chick he cheated on me with. Ain't nothing worse than seeing your man's ex, next, or current side chick when you aren't on your A game.

As soon as I stepped out of the car and thanked him for opening the door for me, he pushed me up against it and kissed me lovingly. I was stuck still for a moment in shock, only able to blink my eyes trying to make sure my vision wasn't failing me. I pinched myself to see if I'd wake up in our bed alone. Charles had never been big on public affection, but he was starting off our night with tons of it. I wanted to ask him who he was and what he did with my husband, but I didn't want to ruin the mood.

"Are you ready, Mrs. Bivens?" he asked with a sly smile on his face, knowing I was eating up all of the love he was finally throwing my way.

"You know I am, Mr. Bivens," I all too happily replied.

The restaurant was packed as usual, but I was happy about that. I wanted as many people as possible to see me on Charles's arm, very much in love and still a token in his life. The more eyes that witnessed us meant the more mouths that could run back the news. My last name was still my last name, and it wasn't going to change. I was stuck to him like glue as he led me to the reserved section where his work party was.

"Hey, Charles," one of his many associates spoke, lifting a glass of liquor up in the air.

"My man," Charles spoke back. "You remember my wife Mary, right?" Putting his hand on the small of my back, he pushed me forward some so I could stand next to him instead of behind him. I was used to falling back and playing the backbone to Charles.

"Wow, it has been a while, but I do. You look beautiful, Mary," he spoke to me, grabbing my hand and kissing it. "Once my wife comes off the dance floor with a few of the other wives, I'll introduce you two." He was very friendly, or drunk.

"Great. That would be nice to have a little company once you fellas link up for some drinks and beers." I was being sociable.

"Yeah, because I owe this man a few drinks for saving my ass with the boss last week." He patted Charles on the back. "If it weren't for your husband here, I wouldn't be here now." His words were starting to slur. The whole time he'd been talking to us, he'd been sipping as well.

"All right, man. You're good. We're good. Go on and get back to the party," Charles rushed him away. "We'll catch up later."

"Okay, I see you weren't exaggerating when you said your associates get lit." I laughed.

"I hoped I was wrong, but to make sure we don't stand out, let's play catch up. What shall I get you from the bar, beautiful?"

"I'll start with a peach margarita." I puckered my lips and kissed his cheek. "Thanks for bringing me."

"Thanks for giving us a chance."

I felt like I was back in college again, holding on to my Prince Charming. Charles hadn't taken his eyes off me all night and was now hugged up on me. This was how it used to be when we dated before I got pregnant with Clifton. We were drinking freely, dancing freely, and laughing at absolutely nothing but just because I was in a good head space. Charles was charming me, and I was accepting all of him with open arms.

I smiled at all of his team, putting on the front that we were the happiest couple in the world. Regardless of what we'd been through, I'd invested too much of my time helping Charles build his reputation and career to want to tear it down. As long as he thrived financially, I would thrive financially, because I was straight coming for my cut if I got served divorce papers.

The night was going great until I looked up and saw Mahogany staring at me. I froze and struggled to keep a straight face as I looked her dead in the eye.

Mahogany

Here I was getting the short end of the stick. It seemed like I was getting played and fucked by love once again. Dabbing my eyes with a piece of Kleenex, I was thankful for the final few tears that were falling because I'd already gone through a tsunami of them for what seemed like hours. Each time they dried up, they started right up again. All it took was for me to look at the woman I'd been loving on cuddled up with the man she was still married to. Even now that I was tucked away in my lonely-ass apartment, I had enough sad memories to fuel my bitterness.

I'd been getting fed a completely different story from what Mary had been feeding me. Sitting only a few feet from them, the truth hit me hard as I witnessed them be the couple she promised me they weren't. My stomach was tied up in knots watching her be in love with someone else. Whereas she'd told me she wasn't happy with that Charles character any longer and that he made her skin cringe, I couldn't tell that from the humungous grin on her face. The feeling of being used overwhelmed me, to the point of wanting revenge.

I'd gone to the restaurant she and I went to for our first date for my called-in order, and I saw them snuggled up outside by the fireplace, only a few booths away from where we'd dined. I was mad at myself for not knowing any better. I was disappointed in myself for believing any

of the stories she'd told me about him. I was angry at myself for being a fool. A big part of me wanted to rush up
to their table and blow up her little party, putting all her
lesbian affair with me on the spot for everyone to judge.
But being weak, I didn't. I'd needed to get my feelings in
control and position myself into the point of power.

Kandace

I'd been wanting to throw up since Charles dragged
his mutt through the door of the place. Even with us
beefing, he was wrong as hell for flaunting her around
me. What damn nerve and big balls his ass had. I was
heated, to say the least. I swear to God I wanted to throw
up in my damn mouth. A big part of me wanted to leave
the party early and go fuck their house up or something,
but I couldn't stop watching the two of them. Even with
them making me want to throw up I still could not bring
myself to look away. It was like one of those "train wrecks
destined to happen" types of things people often spoke of.

His mule-face wife kept smiling and giggling like they
were the happiest husband and wife team in the world
when, just two weeks ago, that man was all up inside of
me. It was taking everything in me not to jump up and
expose them both but especially Charles. He was lucky
that I needed for him to keep his job. I had to remove myself temporarily from what I was seeing and quick before
I snapped.

Going into the bathroom, I locked myself into a stall
and pulled a roll of thirteen pictures out of my purse.
Since it was absolutely clear I wasn't going to get my man,
I moved on to plan B, which was to get some money out
of him instead. Sending all thirteen pictures to Charles's

cell along with a short snippet of a video, I gave him seventy-hours to pay me or I was going to send the same photos to his wife. *You've gotta watch who you mess with because a bitter bitch will jump on a mission to ruin your life.*

Mary Bivens

I didn't know what to do when I saw Mahogany standing before me, so I stood still and acted like both of us were invisible. For everything I'd told her about Charles, how I was miserable and that I was going to leave him and be with her, that all seemed like blatant lies now I was sure. I felt terrible. I wanted to cut through the crowd and apologize for everything, but I couldn't. Not being here with Charles and for his job. My heart felt a little lighter when she walked away without causing a scene, but it was now filled up with worry.

"Babe, are you okay?" Charles asked with concern in his voice, obviously noticing that I'd changed and started distancing myself from the evening. I could tell I was spaced out within my thoughts.

"Yeah, I'm good. I think I might've just had a little bit too much to drink," I tried playing it off, which was a very good excuse because we'd been drinking like fish.

"Do you want to sit down and I can go grab you a bottle of water?" he asked, placing his arm on my back to make sure I could stand up.

I acted a little off balance on purpose, but I was fine. I just needed a few seconds alone to send an "I'm sorry" text message to Mahogany. "Yes, please; both great ideas."

After making sure I was settled at one of the booths, he darted out of the section we were sat in, toward the bar. As soon I couldn't see him anymore, I pulled out my phone and started typing a text message to Mahogany crazily fast. Every few sentences, I restated that I was sorry. I hit SEND as soon as I was done but I kept my phone in the palm of my hand. I wanted to see the checkmark beside the message so I would know she read it. That checkmark didn't pop up, though. I couldn't get any reception where I was sitting so the messages wouldn't go through. I got up and went to the bathroom. I had to pee anyway.

Charles Bivens

"Hey, my man. Can I get two bottles of water when you get a chance?"

"Yup, sure thing. Coming right up." He took my four dollars and moved to the icebox that was at the other side of the bar. Everything about tonight had been going good. Mary looked radiant on my shoulder, we were having a great time, and even Kandace was on her best behavior. Or so I thought she was until I started getting back-to-back text messages. Each one that came through made me lose my breath more and more. This little trick was getting more brazen and ridiculous than I thought she could be. Lastly, this dirty, conniving, good-for-nothing tramp even sent me a video she had. Hitting DIAL on my phone, I was mad as fuck. I wanted nothing more than to stomp two mud holes in this bitch.

"Hey, Charlie, baby," Kandace answered, antagonizing me like she couldn't get dealt with.

"Where are you at in this damn club? I know you some-where near so don't front," I cut straight to the chase, ready to grab a bottle from behind the bar and slam it over her head.

"Who, me? Front? Never that. I'm in the bathroom, bae. I felt little queasy to my stomach." I thought she called herself being funny. "Why? Are you going to come in here and fuck me while your precious Mary waits on the dance floor for you to get finish with this good pussy you know I got? Or are you gonna send her in here to see about me like a good little nursemaid?"

"Yo, girl, are you crazy or something?" I fired back, try-ing not to get loud.

"Yup, crazy for you, daddy big dick who's married to Mary's ass who out there looking like an old piece of shit on a stick," she swiftly answered, not holding me up on speaking about my better half.

"Look, you dumb bitch, your best bet is to leave my wife's name out your mouth."

"I bet that I will not," she growled, following it up with a threat. "And if you don't want me to tell your wife, you better come up with some cash. I'm still salty over how you didn't leave any money for me that day, and you knew I needed to pay my bill."

"Kandace, I don't know why you're doing this, but you better think long and hard, then stop. I'm telling you right here and now I can create the type of problems you re-ally and truly do not want to deal with. Now I have been trying my best to let you have your little tantrums and whatnot, but all these back-to-back texts, pictures, your little video, and your petty threats pertaining to me and mine have worn on my last damn nerve. You're barking up the wrong tree, youngster. You have no worldly idea who you're dealing with or what I'm capable of." I was calm now but wasn't going to be for long.

"What you capable of? Are you serious right now? You the one who's got the most shit to lose in this situation, not me. So do whatever you think you gotta do. All I know is you got seventy-two hours, playboy; now bye." She ignored me and hung up. I knew she was meaning every single word she had just said, but that would be her mistake if she followed through with exposing this bullshit to Mary. I would deal with that fool later. I had other issues on my plate and bigger fish to fry.

My wife was waiting for me and this night belonged to her and me. Unfortunately, by the time I went back to the bar, got Mary's water, and returned to the table, she was gone. Here I was standing there looking lost until one of my associates said she had called an Uber and abruptly left.

Chapter Seventeen

Mary Bivens

I'd gotten up, cooked breakfast, and even eaten my portion by the time Charles walked into the kitchen with his head dropped low. "Good morning," I greeted him first, putting on a fake chipper voice and a fake chipper smile.

"Good morning." The tone of his voice was as low as his head was dropped. "I'm shocked you even cooked. Hell, I am shocked you are still here."

"Why? Because I told you I did not want to be surprised by another woman jumping out of your damn closet?" I was being passive aggressive and didn't care one bit.

He kept his lips sealed, knowing there was no way to explain what I'd heard while in the stall next to his secretary. Kandace has been sucking my husband's dick and then fixing her funny-looking mouth to smile at me for months. It was not enough for him to stop sleeping with her. I wanted her thirsty ass to die from dehydration. I wanted her ass in the unemployment line. Fixing Charles a full plate of food, I set it in front of him and then sat across from him like a ruler. I didn't know if it was me having access to his account or me getting my pussy stroked tenderly that had my ego so swollen, but it was, and I was about to act on those feelings.

"Whatever bullshit you planned on feeding me, save it and wash your food down with it. I'm not worried about when y'all dated because I know y'all are done dating. And to ensure that rotten-face whore understands how done y'all are, I want her fired. Are we clear or what?"

"Mary, I can't." He was much too quick to reply with his refusal for my liking.

I took a deep breath and counted to ten not once but twice. I had to control myself from flipping the hot plate of food over into his lap. "What? You must have thought me telling you to get rid of her stank ass was an option. It was not." I was firm.

Taking a deep breath like I had just done, Charles shook his head and then tried holding hands with me from across the table. I pushed his hands back. He could keep his con man player tactics and use them on one of his sluts he insisted on keeping time with.

"Naw, Charles. Keep your hands. We've been holding hands, kissing, and playing like shit is sweet for weeks. What did all of that mean? I'll tell you what it means. That I've been bamboozled by your cheating ass again." I was hotter than fish grease, ready to pop and burn his ass.

"But, Mary, it is not what you think. I have not messed around with that girl since before you and I started over. I swear. And I tried to get her fired back when I stopped fucking with her but I couldn't."

"You couldn't? Why not? Who is she? The owner's daughter or some shit like that?"

It took him few seconds to respond. "Naw, Mary."

"Then what? You better hurry up and start talking before I go down to that office and start asking the questions I want answers to."

"Because of the great reviews I've given her while she's been there, I really don't have a leg to stand on to fire her. And since I've stopped banging her, she's gotten friendlier with other people within the company who can stop whatever firing I start."

"Wow, now ain't this some disrespectful, foul shit? Am I supposed to be stuck with the feeling of anxiety that you're fucking that bitch while you're supposed to be working every single day? It is already bad enough that you had both of us in the same place."

"I promise you, Mary, I am not messing with her anymore. You have nothing to worry about."

"But you do," I growled. "I have taken a lot of garbage from you that no other woman in the entire world would even think of taking off of you. But what I will not tolerate is you working side by side with a woman you've had sex with. If she can't be replaced, then you need to let them know they need to replace you."

"Whoa, whoa, whoa. Wait." He got loud hoping that I might back down like I had always done in the past. "I just can't up and quit my damn job out of the blue. Be sensible."

"Look, Charles, you can, and you better."

"Am I supposed to take that as a threat? I've already told you what is up and how my hands are tied. I'm not lying, Mary. For real."

His words were falling on deaf ears. "You can take it how you want to take it, Charles. And you can also act on it the way you want to act on it. Just know that every step of the way, I mean you can, and you better."

Getting up from the table, I walked away from it and out of the kitchen, not looking back at him over my shoulder. I did not need a response, a reaction, or a bullshit-ass retort that I wouldn't be accepting anyway. I wanted that woman gone, and I was not accepting anything else.

I was in the den on my laptop when Charles left for work. He'd tried coming to the door and knocking on it, in hopes that I would take my ultimatum off the table, but I kept it locked and refused to answer or budge on what I wanted. For all I had accepted and dealt with, Charles owed me, and I was not counting up the dollars within his bank account to get my payback. I'd heard the way she talked to him, and I didn't like it. Charles might not have been messing with her now, but when he was, that shit was serious. I was no fool.

For the entire morning, I researched Kandace. I looked on every reputable site I could for some information on her, including the white pages and LinkedIn. I then searched for her on social media. Not only did I want her unemployed, but I wanted access to her outside of that job. I had every intention of making her pay on several different levels for coming for me. Kandace should have stayed clear of me instead of trying to manipulate my business. Her fooling me for eight months was what had me most upset. She could have slept with him and left me out of it.

Charles Bivens

Going over the same set of codes for the fifth time, I couldn't focus on work because I was too busy thinking of Mary's ultimatum. I did not blame her for wanting Kandace gone, but I was upset with her for not listening to my reasons about how her demand was not possible, especially with the girl being pregnant. I was just glad Mary didn't know that part. I probably wouldn't be sitting here and living right now. *"If she can't be replaced, then you need to let them know they will need to replace you."* My wife's words kept playing over and over again in my mental.

Mary was so adamant on separating Kandace and me that she was willing to put me on the chopping block at work. She was basically telling me to jump off a cliff and hope not to fall. For the sake of mending her heart and giving her peace of mind, it was worth my reputation to her. Not to me, however. I wasn't in a bad predicament. I was in a no-win situation. I did not have a valid reason to terminate Kandace, and the higher-ups could quite possibly launch an investigation if I requested her termination again because it would seem suspicious given the first experience and outcome. I was stuck between a rock and a hard place, afraid that all my past was coming back to kill me, fuck haunt me.

I jumped when my cell rang, which was a dead sign that I was on edge and nervous. I didn't want Mary to waltz up in here and create a domino effect of negative scenes. Anyway, the caller was my daughter. I quickly answered because I hadn't talked to her since we fell out about school and that boy. Though she'd been wrong as two left shoes, I missed my baby girl.

"Hey, Melissa."

"Hey, Dad."

She paused for a few and then started explaining herself. Melissa went right in giving her father the current update with her schooling. She knew she had let him down over the past few months. Having been his little spoiled princess her entire life, she wanted to make sure he knew that no matter what, he was appreciated.

By the time the heartfelt conversation could draw to an end, the tables somehow turned. Charles was no longer listening to his daughter tell her truths; he was now telling his own. Confessing that things had gotten totally off track with him and her mother, he let her know that it was on him. Charles took all the blame saying not one thing wrong that Mary had done.

Like most kids, Melissa wanted to see her parents stay together. With the aid of Google, she searched for a few nearby getaway spots. Happily, she forwarded the information to her dad, hoping for the family's sake he would follow through on his vow to make things right with her mother, his wife.

Mary Bivens

Spending a few hours researching Kandace, I had every intention of taking a long, hot shower and taking a nap; but Charles had other plans. He came through door with a large bouquet of red roses and a bunch of bags. I shot him a few eye daggers. If he thought he could buy my anger, embarrassment, and hurt off with some damn flowers, he must have been sick in the head.

Charles Bivens

"Hey, baby." I walked over to Mary and placed a wet kiss on her mouth.

"Charles, what is all this for? I didn't want a bunch of gifts. All I wanted to hear was that you got rid of that damn girl. Now, what's the damn status on that?"

"I put in the word to human resources," I lied, hoping she bought it so I could have a little more time to get things together.

"Good. Great. Wonderful. Now if you can't work without an assistant like you claim, then I'll be your assistant, case closed."

"Sweetie, that's not a problem. We'll get the ball rolling on that," I lied through my teeth, willing to say anything to appease her. Not too proud to beg, I got down on one knee and gave Mary a small bag with a box inside. It wasn't hard for her to figure out what it was, but still, she seemed not to be moved. Even after opening it and me saying that it was a new wedding ring signifying my new commitment to our marriage, Mary gave me the side-eye. I didn't let her apprehensive demeanor stop me from announcing that we would be going on a quick getaway spa resort where we could renew our vows. I made sure to throw in the part about our loving daughter being the one to suggest it. I knew Mary would do anything to make our kids happy.

Chapter Eighteen

Mary Bivens

I was in my feelings like a muthafucka as he was on my heels up the stairs to our bedroom. I didn't know if he was actually attracted to me right now in the moment or was thinking about all the things I finally told him I had done with the next female. I told him on our spa getaway after we renewed our vows.

Charles was a true freak. He hadn't come for me like this since the night we made Clifton. His hands were on a trip all over my body. I couldn't keep them from grabbing on my hips and my backside.

As soon as we hit the bedroom door, he pushed me through it and toward the bed. Off came his shirt. He started undoing his belt and pants zipper, too. "Are you going to lick on this dick the same way I know you licked on ol' girl's kitty cat? I can't lie and say I'm not a little bit jealous about you giving her head like I know you did. That shit had to be so erotic and hot as hell." He wasn't looking at me weirdly or differently because I'd caressed on, kissed on, and even gone down on Mahogany. Charles was turned on by all that I'd done to her, and he wanted his chance to get the same, if not more.

"Do me a favor and dress in black," he begged, panting and kissing all over my cleavage.

Blushing and giggling, I was happy to oblige my man. I was even happier that he'd been turned on and attracted to me still after all we'd been through and all the women he'd dealt with. "Your wish is my command, baby. I can most definitely dress up for you. Go downstairs and grab us something to drink and I'll start getting ready."

"Hell yeah. I'll be right back." He excitedly left the room and headed downstairs.

Hurrying around the room, I grabbed a few outfits out of my drawer to pick from and a neutral pair of heels. I wasn't going to wear the same getups I'd worn at the resort, but something fresh and new. I even grabbed a few props: my whip, some cuffs, and some massage oil. I was excited about getting to test out a few new things with Charles. Tonight was definitely a full night of firsts for me.

I took a three-minute shower, applied some vanilla body cream to my skin, and slid on a cute little police officer's lingerie set. The idea to punish Charles for all of his unfaithful ways crossed and stuck with my mind. I even planned on using the prop handcuffs I'd purchased from the novelty store to restrain him. Since role playing was what he requested, it was what he would get.

By the time I walked back into our room, Charles was posted in the bed with his back against the headboard and hand wrapped around his semi-hard cock. "Damn, you look good as hell, woman," he complimented me as his hands eyes traced my body, undressing me from what little material I had on. "I'm really digging these surprises you keep coming at me with."

"Really?" I asked, trying to sound innocent yet seductive at the same time.

"Hell yeah, really. You're gonna have to dress up for your husband more often." Charles would've been drooling had he not been biting his lip so hard.

Though I didn't have any music to dance to, I caught a beat in my head and danced over to him. His hands were waiting anxiously to touch me again, and that they did. I almost climaxed off him rubbing me the right way. Climbing onto the bed, I straddled him, but with my back toward his face so he could get a good view of my pink pussy. I wanted all of his attention to be focused there.

On cue, he started a sixty-nine position pleaser by tickling my clitoris with his tongue while pushing my head down onto his dick. I opened my mouth and let his dick slide down my tongue and throat as far as it would go; then I lifted his hips so it would slide even farther down my throat. I was willing to go for the gusto with my husband tonight, regardless of his mushroom tip blocking my airway or the tears coming from my eyes because of that. Yup, even the thought of that actually meaning something again made me hornier.

As soon as I got the hang of the head job I was giving him, he pulled it out and lifted me up over his erection. Holding my hips tightly, he got a steady rhythm going as he stroked himself deeper and deeper into me. I was shaking, and the arch in my back ached from how he'd gotten into me. I was losing control as he neared my G-spot. Cupping and palming my breasts, I tilted my head back like the girls do in the movies, and he leaned over and sucked on my neck. It felt like he was leaving hickeys.

"Don't leave any marks on me, Charles." I felt like I was too old to have passion marks on me. And that it would be embarrassing for Melissa and Clifton to see.

"I'm your husband. I can leave what I want on you." He'd said the magic word that made everything seem better for me: husband.

I started going crazy on his dick, pouncing up and down on it like I was on a pogo stick. The length, thickness, and veins of it felt good against my slippery walls. When I slowed down to catch my breath, Charles took control again by spreading the lips of my pussy and cir-

cling my clit with his thump until I jumped with energy
again. Then he started stroking me again. I damn near
passed out from all the separate stimulations happening
all at once. It seemed that Mahogany had taught both of
us something. Charles was now aiming to sexually please
me.

"I'm about to pass out. Oh my God, this feels so good."
I was panting.

"Turn around and stay straddled. This is my pussy tonight." There was something about the way he said it that
turned me on even more.

Spinning around, I started riding him, but I was most-
ly guided by his hands being on my hips. I was not sure
why, but he felt deeper, and each stroke was more intense. I couldn't compete as far as adrenaline went, but
I kept contracting my pussy walls to help him keep his
adrenaline up. We both seemed hungry and desperate for
one another.

"Is it good for you?" I moaned.

"Yes, fuck yes," he grunted. "Don't stop riding this dick,
girl." Spreading my cheeks, he put his finger into my booty hole and drilled into me until I started spinning on his
dick.

I couldn't do anything but grab a hold of his back to
help brace myself and take it. He wasn't showing me any
mercy, and I refused to show any weakness. We both
wanted to cum.

"Is it mine, Mary?" he asked, panting and trying to pull
me even farther down on him, as if that was going to in-
fluence my answer.

"Yes, baby. All of me is yours. Always has been. Always
will be."

"Good answer." He started passionately kissing me.

We kept touching, fucking, loving, and kissing on one
another for a couple more minutes before the intensity

turned too far up. My legs were trembling and felt numb by the time I fell off his lap onto the bed. The explosion he made my body go through leveled me for sleep.

My eyes popped open a few hours later, in the middle of the night. I was lying across Charles in a puddle of our sweat and cum. We'd both fallen asleep right afterward and hadn't cleaned up. For a few minutes, I lay still and danced over the thoughts of our sex session to the sound of his heartbeat until all the negative feelings about all the women he'd slept with started pouring into my mind. That's when I slipped out of bed and took his phone into the bathroom with me.

As soon as I picked up Charles's phone, it felt like I was supposed to put it back down and not cause myself any additional stress. But at the same time, I could not pass up the opportunity to find out what had really been going on in his world. His cell phone to him was like the Bible to Christians. It held all the sacred truths.

After punching in the code to unlock it, I went straight to his text messages. Out of every application, that was the one to tell me who, what, when, and where. The more I scrolled through them, the nuttier I felt. And when I got to a video message from Kandace of her at the doctor getting a sonogram, I slammed it into porcelain sink until the entire screen shattered and the phone was ruined. I had to hurry up and get out of the house before I literally killed Charles.

I was fuming. I couldn't believe I thought this lying sack of shit was telling the truth. I should have known better than to forgive him. I needed to stop trusting this asshole and go be with someone who cared about me and had my best interests at heart: Mahogany.

Chapter Nineteen

Mary Bivens

I was beside myself. I had not been this mad or this disappointed in Charles in years. As I sat in my car, I couldn't help but close my eyes and think of all the low-down, dirty things he had done to me throughout the years. *Damn.*

It was raining. Huge downpours of showers flooded the roads. There was lightning. Repeatedly, the sky brightly lit up, then returned to utter darkness. The earsplitting sounds of car alarms being set off were countless. Strong, twisting winds and thunder rattled windows. This was that extreme weather most people traveling the streets at this time of night or day hated to have occur. That eerie, "goose bumps and chills and something bad was bound to happen" weather. It was three thirty-four in the early morning hours, the time most heinous crimes were committed, drunk drivers coming from the club, car crashes, loyal wives at home sitting by the window wondering where their rotten piece-of-shit husbands are. The thought took me back to a night just like this one.

Life had just gotten as real as it possibly could for Mary Bivens as she could not wait, gazing out that foggy window behind her expensive sheer curtains. Despite being terrified, nervous, and in excruciating pain, the stay-at-home wife, very much in labor, went to the car and attempted to drive herself to the hospital. Besides the baby fighting aggressively to get out of her stomach, she was solo. Without her child's sperm donor dad by her side, Mary bossed up.

No doubt he was relaxing at some strip club or with one of his various bitches who were itching to come out of the shadows. The dedicated wife still had her dignity and continued to play her position. This incident, although once in a lifetime, was no different from the other numerous occasions throughout the years she'd been forced to do whatever she needed to do for the family. Mary wished all the no-good home-wrecking side chicks knew the grief they caused others when messing around with the next person's husband. But no, that would be too much like right for them to just find their own man and leave what could be happy families alone. Mary wished there were a law against cheating; although, if that was the case, her husband would be locked away behind bars doing life without any chance of parole.

Having no options or real friends she could count on, including Charles's no-good self as of late, she did what had to be done. As the windshield wipers went back and forth, she fretfully bit down on the corner of her Botox-filled lower lip. The expectant mother dodged fallen tree limbs scattered about. Gripping the steering wheel, she swerved around several stalled vehicles, almost sideswiping one.

Her tank was on E. Mary was forced to get five dollars in gas, and she even managed to pump it herself. She wanted nothing more than to call Charles once more and beg him to come home, but she knew he was not picking up. Mrs. Bivens knew the games her once loyal husband was playing and the life she chose sticking by him in good times and bad. So she shook off that notion of swallowing her pride by tapping the redial button and pushed on.

What should have been a ten-minute drive turned into twenty as the weather conditions intensified. Avoiding hitting one stray dog and two black long-tail squirrels, Mary finally made it to her destination. She had fought the storm and won. Smashing her designer flip-flop down onto the brake pedal, her ankles swollen in their size sevens, all four wheels screeched, locking up.

Double-parking the small SUV, she took a deep breath as the ongoing contractions kicked into major overdrive. This time they were more intense than the others. Frantic, Mary screamed out as her water broke, soaking the entire driver's seat. Now clothed in a sundress whose lower area was drenched, she prayed for the best and gathered more courage.

Fleeing the vehicle, the house wife abandoned it, not once looking back. The hazard lights were left flashing as if the truck were an ambulance on a 911 mission. Wobbling through the slightly tinted glass doors of the emergency room entrance, she held her protruding belly. Face full of tears streaming down both cheeks, Mary pleaded to the guards to let her through the security checkpoints without getting properly searched.

She got a stern response. "All right, look, miss, I can clearly see you are in pain. And whereas I do sympathize with you, that vehicle you were driving has to be moved, now. Our policy is strict around here. It forbids any vehicles to be in that zone no longer than a few minutes for emergency drop-off or pick-up only."

"Yeah, okay, and—"

"And like I said, once again, miss, your vehicle has to be moved." He nodded his head toward the door while reaching for his radio. "And I mean right now before we have to have it towed. The designated company we use is on twenty-four-hour call just in case. So please do as we asked you."

"Tow? For real? Oh my God, are you blind or something? I'm pregnant! Can't you see I'm in labor?" she angrily shouted while wiping away the tears with her forearm. *"My water just broke, and I think I'm about to deliver my baby. I don't have time to think shit about parking no damn truck."* Mary glanced over her shoulder at her illegally parked SUV then back at the guard. Her usual womanly charms were not working on the opposite sex, not tonight. Maybe it was her triple-size swollen belly, her weather-drenched, matted hair, or no perfectly applied makeup. Nevertheless, whatever it was, the magic Mary often relied on to get men to give into her whims was missing. Just like Charles had stop finding her attractive and paid her no mind, these men must have been cut from that same *"fuck Mary Bivens"* cloth.

Distressed, her eyes then darted over toward the nurses' triage station that was located only a few yards away from where she was. Suffering from yet another grueling sharp contraction, the mother-to-be doubled over, panting to catch her breath. She wanted to pass out. Both legs were weakening as the baby inside of her was ready to see daylight. The assistance she required so desperately was right there. A part of Mary's arrogant upbringing wanted her to say to hell with the world and its rules and make a dash for it. Whereas the other part knew she was in a no-win situation.

"Damn, are y'all freaking serious right about now? I need help." She used both hands to clutch her stomach as her wet clothes stuck to her body.

The guard closest to the metal detector was now on his feet waiting for Mary to try anything unexpected. He must have seen the desperation brewing in her eyes. Backing down, Charles's wife turned, heading to the same door she'd just come in, preparing herself to brave the elements and find somewhere allowable to park.

"Hey, Mary, girl. What's happening? You good over there or what?"

Turning to see a familiar face, Mary paused then exhaled. Any other time, she would be annoyed as hell having to see or even speak to this certain individual. But this time she was relieved and threw no shade. This time the annoying female's presence was welcomed. Leesa, who also appeared to be with child, had grown up in the same neighborhood as Mary did, although they never ran in the same circles.

Definitely not cut from the same cloth, Mary and her once small, close-knit circle of nice schoolgirls was everything Leesa and her friends weren't. Leesa had always been slightly overweight, wearing clothes that were out of style and walked around with a negative disposition because of it. Yet that wasn't the true difference between the two. The fact that Mary, also slightly overweight, wanted to do the right thing and keep her legs closed until the right man came along made them opposites. But, hot in the pants, Leesa didn't give a damn about right or wrong or waiting. She had no problem whatsoever trying to get with the next female's boyfriend.

Mary didn't like that flawed character trait and, since childhood, she had no problem letting it be known. She'd heard through the grapevine that Leesa had more than likely messed around with somebody else's man and was knocked up from that. Sadly, for all she knew, this dedicated side piece tramp was pregnant by Charles as well. This was the first time she had seen the neighborhood floozy face to face in well over a year or so since an impromptu sighting at the mall. And judging from her view, the old neighborhood gossip intel was obviously true.

"Oh, hey, Leesa." Mary removed her hand, clad in a huge diamond ring, from her stomach. Whereas part of her wanted to just throw up in her mouth from the way Leesa looked, the other part needed a solid. So, of course, Mary played nice. "I'm so glad to see someone I know. Can you please help me?"

Immediately Mary noticed a strange look come over her face. It was a look of, "Finally, you uppity bitch, you need something from me. Me, the girl you and your college-bound friends used to ridicule, judge, and look down on for doing what I had to do."

After a few brief seconds of dead silence, Leesa responded, "Yeah, okay, Mary, no problem. What you need, girlfriend? I'm here for you, especially since we seem to be in the same family way."

Mary wanted to yell. She wanted to scream. She wanted to tell everyone listening within ear range that this tack-head hood rat was nothing like her. She wanted them to know that other than the zip code they once shared as children, Leesa's man-borrowing butt was out of Mary's league. But, instead, she chilled.

"Look, sis." She sarcastically smiled the best she could, considering the physical pain she was in because of a baby on the verge of busting through her innards and the mental anguish she was suffering from the absence of her husband, the great Charles Bivens. "You think you can move my truck for me out of their emergency ambulance lane? I don't think I can make it back out there. I think my baby is coming."

Once again, Leesa gave her the "bitch, really" eye, but reached her hands out for the keys just the same. Trying to look, but not look at the same time, Mary saw blatant needle tracks down her arm. She had heard she was out in the streets doing more than messing around with married men, but now she saw the evidence first-hand.

Now her messy appearance made perfect sense. Mary knew she was in labor and had driven through damn near hurricane weather and almost got struck by lightning while pumping gas. That's why she looked a hot mess; but, Leesa, her excuse was dope.

A part of Mary felt sorry for her "side chick from birth" ass, but the other part said she got no worse than the karma she deserved. Mary was glad she was smart enough to choose school over a man; even though, truth be told, where did it get her? Standing in the middle of the emergency room, side by side, big belly by big belly, alone with no baby daddy by her side just like this drug addict dopehead.

Mary shook off her vindictive emotions focused on Leesa whatever her last name was, and she got them back where they belonged: on her unborn child. Turning back to the two stubborn security guards on duty, she told them to just do their job, call the tow truck, and let her through. She would much rather take her chances getting the vehicle impounded and see it again in one piece than have risk have Leesa drive off and take the SUV to the local chop shop. As the guards obliged, they let Mary through the checkpoint. She never once looked back at Leesa. She would not be smoking crack or shooting up off her truck's vital organs.

Throughout the entire wing of the hospital floor, it was quiet except for Mother Nature doing her thing and of course a very married but still very alone Mrs. Charles Bivens screaming out for God to show her mercy for the pain she was suffering. Already short staffed because of budget cuts and the awful weather, a skeleton crew maintained the best they possibly could. Mary wanted her own doctor to be present, but he was still out of the country on some sort of business seminar. She knew if Charles were here he would at least make them

*get her the best physicians they had or at least make
her feel confident. But he wasn't; she was here solo. She
didn't sign up for this life, but she was in the middle of
playing the cards she was dealt.*

*"Okay great, miss, you're doing well. Now relax," the
young-looking doctor on staff coaxed, never once lifting
his head. "Take two short but deep breaths then push a
little harder. We are definitely seeing the head. Nurse,
nurse, something is wrong. Grab those biceps."*

*Those were the last words Mary heard before she
passed out cold.*

*What she knew was that, hours later, she awoke to
being in a hospital bed with several IVs in her arms
and a clear plastic line of oxygen in both of her nostrils.
Groggily she tried to get up, but she was much too weak.
Seconds later a nurse came into the room with a chart
in her hand.*

*"Excuse me, nurse, excuse me. I had my baby last
night. Can you please get my baby? Where is my baby?
Please bring me my baby! Now! Please!"*

A horn blowing brought me back to attention from the
God-awful flashback I was having. I'd almost crashed
the car. I had chills even thinking about the memory of
that night I had buried deep in the rear of my mind. Not
only had I gone through the terrible misfortune of giving
birth to baby who strangled himself to death with his
umbilical cord, but Charles didn't show up to comfort me
or mourn the loss of our baby until later that afternoon.
And I knew he had been with another women that day because he didn't even have the decency to wash her cheap
scent off his shirt.

Pulling into the hotel room I planned on crashing at for
a while, I hoped they didn't find my body in here behind
a suicide. 'Cause I was surely going to take a mouthful of
antidepressants when I walked through the door.

Chapter Twenty

Mahogany

Curled up with Jasmine, I didn't know where my skin ended and where hers started. We made love all night. I could tell from how hard she'd been stroking me with the dildo that she'd been trying to get me stuck. Stuck back in love with her. Stuck back going crazy over her. And stuck to the point that I couldn't even have feelings for another woman. Jasmine hated Mary. She couldn't believe I'd let someone into the heart she'd been holding captive for years. But I had. And I was missing Mary like an addict misses his craving on the first day of detox. It was killing me that we hadn't spoken in days.

I was hating myself for not being able to shake Mary's trifling ass, but I couldn't stop myself from thinking about her. In the short amount of time of us messing around with one another, I'd grown to have a passionate attraction and love for her that I couldn't explain. I thought I'd successfully turned her out, but it was starting to seem like I had gotten pussy whipped.

Unhooking myself from Jasmine, I softly kissed her forehead before slipping out of the bed. Despite her sexiness, I couldn't stay wrapped up with her while my mind was racing about another woman. A part of me wished I would have given myself some time to heal instead of slipping my tongue into her panties.

First picking up all the clothes Jasmine stripped out of coming in my crib, I then started pacing my living room floor with my phone in my hand. I wanted to call Mary, but her not answering my call would hurt worse than not knowing if she would answer my calls. I was conflicted. After going back and forth with it in my mind and then flipping a coin, I hit SEND on my cell and hoped she answered on her end. My nerves were racked, especially when it got to the third ring. I almost hung up.

"Hello." She sounded like she couldn't believe my name and number was on her screen. My heart fluttered.

"Wow, it's so good to hear your voice," I spoke into the phone, unfamiliar with my own voice because it was high-pitched and scratchy.

"Yours too," she responded. "I didn't think I'd hear from you after what happened."

"You weren't going to hear from me again." I was honest but short about the depths of my feelings. "But I couldn't stop thinking about you."

"I've been thinking about you nonstop too, Mahogany. I'm so sorry about everything that has transpired. I swear that I didn't mean for things to go left with us." She was sniffling. "Shit just got out of control so fast. I hadn't expected to fall as hard as I did with you. Nor had I expected Charles to start acting like he wanted our marriage to work. I got confused, scared, and didn't know how to handle it." She poured her emotions out.

"Well, have you figured out what it is or who it is you want? I'm missing you, which is the reason I broke down and called, but I can't keep being your pacifier when Charles makes you mad. I've got feelings too." My voice was cracking.

There was complete silence from both of us. I was deep into my thoughts, trying to figure out what to say next and I was sure she was doing the same thing. Neither one of us wanted to say the wrong thing. Neither one of us wanted to let go, but the situation had gotten so messy. No longer had we been fucking for fun, or meeting up on an everyday basis because Charles was out having play time with whatever flavor of the week he was fucking. We'd been making plans to have a future with one another.

"I love you, Mahogany." She spoke like her words were magic.

"For real, Mary? Do you really? Didn't you love me before? What's so different about then and now?" I wasn't giving her a break. I wanted an answer with some substance. Something I could hold on to.

There was another silence shared between us. From me because I was waiting for Mary to speak up. And from her because she was probably afraid to say the wrong thing.

"Can we start over and only focus on us? Take it back to the carefree and happy times when the only things that mattered were our smiles? If nothing else, I want the friend I had in you back."

"I can't be your friend." I kept it real. "With me and you, it's all or nothing. I can't share you, send you home to him after I fuck you, or have scheduled times to call you. My feelings run way too deep for some shallow shit like that."

"I know you don't have a reason to believe me, but I promise you that it won't be like that. Charles and I aren't even sleeping underneath the same roof." She dropped a bag of news I had no idea about. "I left him, Mahogany. Well, I plan on leaving him."

I was flabbergasted. "What? When? Are you serious?"

"Yeah, I'm serious. I know you are going to say I'm dumb and I deserved to be hurt again, but I broke the code to his phone and found a bunch of messages between him and his secretary. Well, let me correct myself. I found a bunch of messages between him and his baby momma."

I choked on my own saliva. "What in the hell did you just say, Mary? Charles had a baby on you?"

"Not yet, but she's pregnant." I heard the hurt in her voice as she revealed the truth.

"Damn. I wasn't necessarily rooting for the two of you, but you didn't expect that gut punch."

"Right. And that's the part that made me so goddamn angry. I've put up with a lot, but having a kid on me is too much." She started whining even more.

Something inside of me snapped. "So, what are you trying to do? Use me to make you feel better? Use me to give you enough strength to pick your fucking heart up off the ground and put it back together? Are you only apologetic because of what you found out? Don't feed me no bullshit, Mary."

"I'm not. I swear I'm not trying to put you in the middle, use you, or dog you out later. That's why I didn't call you when I left the house." Her voice drifted off, and then I heard her crying heavily in the background.

"Mary. Hey, pick the phone back up. Mary," I called into the phone, almost forgetting that Jasmine was in the back asleep. She wasn't a light sleeper, but not when I was screaming out another woman's name.

A few more seconds passed before Mary picked the phone back up. Her voice was so cracked and tearful it was almost inaudible. "I can understand if you don't believe me, but I really do want to start over with you."

The hold that Mary had over me the first day we started kicking it with one another was the same hold she had over me today. I wasn't able to tell her no. I wanted to comfort her. I wanted her to stay away from Charles. I wanted to fix her heart.

"Where are you staying at?"

"By the airport." She gave me the hotel's name and her room number.

"Okay. Give me about an hour and I'll be there."

"Be where?" Jasmine's voice sounded off as soon as I hung up the phone.

Not knowing how long she'd been standing there, I didn't bother trying to come up with an excuse to spare her feelings. "Mary's hotel room."

First dropping her head, she then rose it and her hand at the same time. I didn't move quick enough to block her palm from slapping me across the cheek.

"I hate you. I hate you. I fucking hate you," she kept screaming, over and over again. "Why did you invite me over here just to play with my feelings again? You aren't shit, Ebony. All you care about is your fucking self."

I ignored the verbal meltdown she was putting into the air, and I addressed the physical one. "Do not put your hands on me again, Jas."

"I'll put my hands on you over and over again for you lying to me over and over again. I want to show you I know how to count too." Reaching up to slap me again, she was caught off guard when I grabbed her wrist and twisted it until her arm twisted and she yelped out in pain. "Let me go. I swear to God that you better get your hands off me."

"I don't want to put my hands on you, Jas. Trust and believe that I don't. But if I let you go and you come at me again, I'm gonna break yo' ass all the way down to the floor." I meant every word of my threat.

"Let me go," she said again, sounding like she was getting ready to cry.

"I will, Jas. But you better hear me loud and clear about those hands of yours." I restated my position, then freed her from the amateur wrestling grip.

"I cannot wait until karma catches up to your ass," she spat.

"Whatever, girl. Now that I've let you go, can you get your shit and go?" I was mad as hell, and I felt my pressure steadily rising. I knew that if she kept pressing my buttons, I would have to flip. I was only human.

"For real, Ebony? It's like that? After all we've been through? I thought we were working toward something." She sounded distraught. "I've been nothing but loyal and committed to you."

Exhausted with the same argument and conversation, I wasn't fazed by her tears or her feelings. I wanted to say as much mean shit as I could say so she would hurry up and get out of my apartment. "Look, if you bought into a dream, it's because you sold yourself one. I never told you that we were exclusive or that us fucking around off and on would one day make us a couple with a dense past. It's not my fault that you didn't keep shit straight."

Time stopped for a few seconds as we stood in silence locked in an eye war. I could tell through the triple coat of tears and the frown on her face that she was hurt. I wanted to apologize, but I couldn't let her leave here with the hopes of coming back, and I didn't want her back. Our relationship was too tumultuous, murky, and now volatile.

Jasmine ran around my apartment in an emotional frenzy, crying and screaming about how I was selfish and inconsiderate while gathering all of her belongings. I watched quietly, making sure she didn't tear up any of my things and I made sure I didn't antagonize her. I hated watching her look like a helpless child, but I couldn't afford the back-and-forth emotional battle that would come afterward. I loved Jasmine. Which meant I had to love her enough to let her go.

"Ebony, please—"

I cut her off. "Stop. Don't do this, Jasmine. I'm toxic for you and to you." I couldn't fall weak to her tears or how heavy the situation was on me.

Collapsing to the floor, she balled up into a knot and started crying erratically, even grabbing on her chest a few times and whining that she couldn't breathe. Jasmine had been emotional and erratic before, but tonight's emotional meltdown was taking the cake.

Our history and my heart wouldn't let me leave her on the floor. Dropping my head, I walked over to her and tried pulling her up. "Jasmine. Stop crying and get up. You can do this, baby girl." I was careful not to give her hope, but a boost to rise above the meltdown. "Come on now, Jas. Get up." I was trying to be sympathetic, but I should have stayed in my corner and let her roll all over my floor until she passed out from exhaustion while I called the cops. I knew showing her an ounce of emotion was going to set her off in a way I didn't need or want to deal with. I did not think, however, that it was going to go into a full-blown rage.

"Why, Ebony? Why? Why are you doing this to me? What can I do to fix this? I don't want to go. I don't want you to leave and go to her." She was babbling, almost completely incoherent. "Please don't end what we have."

Not willing to tell her what she wanted to hear, I instead wiped at her tears and shook my head to stop mine. It was hard not embracing her. It was hard to see her so broken down over me. It was hard knowing that I'd lost my friend because things between us would never be the same. Jasmine's tears were like emotional strings, and they were tugging at my heart. I truly hated causing her any pain. "You have been everything to me, Jas. I know this shit has you broken down now, but—" I was cut off in midsentence.

Jasmine leaped up with a tearstained face and her hands wide open. Once again, because I was blindsided and not expecting it, she was able to catch contact with my face and scratch the hell out of my cheek. From that point, I commenced kicking her ass all over my living room until finally kicking her out, literally. I put my foot right on top of her back, dropped her garbage bag of belongings beside her head, and dared her to ever put her hands on me again. Jasmine was nowhere to be found when I went back out to leave.

Chapter Twenty-one

Mahogany

My hands were aching as I gripped the steering wheel with fury, pushing my gas pedal to the floor toward the airport. I couldn't wait to fall between Mary's thighs and work out the rest of my frustration. Jasmine had me mad as hell. I knew that I'd hurt her feelings, but it wasn't like I'd lied to her about my feelings for Mary. Her having high hopes for us being back together was not my fault.

Arriving at the hotel, I called in and told Mary I was downstairs. When I got to her door, she opened it dressed in a robe. By the time I crossed the threshold, the robe was off her body and on the floor.

"Damn, I've missed you." I fell into her neck, kissing her softly but hungrily. It should have been against the law how much I was into this woman.

Hugging me back just as tightly, I felt her heart beating as I slid my hands around her hips pulling her closer. She felt and smelled so good. I couldn't wait another minute to get reunited with her body. Pushing her back some, I pinched at her nipples and then dropped my head down to lick and suck on them. She tasted so damn good that my taste buds were tingling.

She was on wobbly legs, so I relieved her completely. I pushing her back onto the bed. She pulled me down on top of her before I got a chance to climb on top of her. She was hungry for me, which made me hungrier for her. It felt like I was home as I lay on top of her body, skin to skin, melting into her curves. It felt like were meant to be together as our breathing synced up. Our energy had linked up.

Planting soft kisses on her stomach, I then started sucking on her breasts and then gently on her nipples. I remembered her not liking it rough, so I was careful to pay attention to that.

I then leaned up and kissed her lips again, all four of them. I'd been thinking about doing this for days. Not even sleeping with Jasmine had scratched the itch. Mary was who I wanted, yearned for and, I thought, loved.

Sliding her panties to the side, I opened her up with my free hand and started devouring her. I had missed her sweet nectar hitting my tongue. I'd missed making her feel good. I knew she was squirming off my tongue, but also because I was blowing her mind. She needed her mind blown. Especially after what Charles had done. One of these days karma was going to catch up to him and fuck him with no Vaseline.

Mary started shaking and hyperventilating. From the many times I'd brought her to pleasure, I could tell what was going to happen next.

Mary Bivens

My walls were contracting nonstop at a rapid pace. She'd just finished circling my belly button with her tongue, like she was doing a dance, then massaged the insides of my thigh with the same intensity yet softness she was so skilled at doing. Mahogany should have taught sex seminars. I was turned out and turned on at the same time. The more she breathed on my clit, flicked my clit, then dove into my hotbox in a rotation, the more she had me getting ready to start shouting for God to take me now.

Every single time I thought it was going to be the last time I'd be in Mahogany's arms, I ended up right back between them. And between her legs, too. Her kisses had slowed me all the way down and her loving had made me forget about the pain and hurt Charles had made me a melting pot for. Tonight, unlike any other night of us having sex, there weren't any props. Just us. This was what I needed.

"Promise me that you will stay here while I go get my clothes and some other personal stuff," I begged of her.

"I can do that, of course. But do you want me to go with you?" I knew part of her wanted to make sure I came back.

"No. It could get messy with my kids but, I promise, I will be back in a few."

"Okay, Mary. Please don't make me regret saying I'll stay."

"I won't, and I'll be right back." I got up to get dressed, though I should have never left her side. At least, not right then anyway.

Chapter Twenty-two

Mary Bivens

I thought I would be able to come to the house to pack a bag of clothes and leave without getting emotional, but I was wrong. I had not been able to control my tears since I walked through my front door. After all I had done fighting for Charles and this marriage, even forgiving him and giving him another chance, I was right back at the point of feeling like I had to give up. I had been crippled from the continuous heartache.

Somewhere in between packing my clothes and crying, I passed out on the bed from exhaustion. By the time I woke up, Charles was pushing our bedroom door open with another bouquet of red roses in his hand. I frowned up my face at him and his weak-ass approach toward an apology. It wasn't going to be as easy as it had been in the past for him to fall back within my good graces. The cuts had gone too deep. Having a child outside of our marriage was much different from having an orgasm. I couldn't push the memory down to be forgotten. And if I did forgive him, the hurt would be too constant. I was fucked up mentally and emotionally.

My body sank into the bed when he sat down beside me. So weak from crying, being fucked by Mahogany, and running through the house gathering all my stuff, I didn't have the energy to move. Charles took the opportunity to apologize while he had it.

"Baby, I know I can never take back all of the hurt I have caused you doing this marriage, but I swear I can fix this."

"Wow, Charles. Really?" I was taken aback by his words and how sincere he sounded.

"Yeah, Mary. I want to be a better husband to you. The type of husband you deserve. That you've always deserved. I know it's hard to believe, but I really do miss us."

Hearing him admit to hurting me and this marriage and then apologize was a bittersweet moment. It felt good to know he loved me and wanted to revitalize what he'd tried killing; but, on the other hand, I couldn't help but be salty because he'd wasted so many of my years with bitches. Bitches who didn't matter now but meant the world to him when he was leaving me lonely.

"Mary, why haven't you answered any of my calls? I've been calling, text messaging. I was even going to have the kids reach out to you for me if it came to that." He had the nerve to sound upset.

Instead of telling him he deserved to know how I'd been feeling for all the years of him stepping out on me, I set it off in another way. "Which kids, Charles? Mine or your ho's baby? I knew that bitch was bad news." I knew the unborn seed couldn't make a phone call, but it fit in perfectly.

He looked defeated. For the first time in twenty years, I actually had Charles speechless.

I giggled. "Yup, you've been cold busted. I know about Charles, Jr. Congratulations." I didn't know if the baby was a boy, but I was trying to be feisty and witty and to keep the tears from falling to show how he'd broken me down. With a snarl on my face, I lifted my hand and smacked the shit out of him. "And I'm telling the kids."

Charles leaped up and grabbed my arm. "Wait a damn minute. This doesn't have to leave this bedroom. Let me explain."

"You better let go of me, Charles," I screamed.

"Please. Mary, you've gotta listen. That girl is trying to trap me with that baby. That's why she sent all those pictures, and that's the tail end of the conversation you heard in the bathroom that night. I swear I'm done with her, and I don't want us to have a kid. I begged her to get an abortion, but she knows I'll be her meal ticket."

"Oh my God," I shouted in disbelief. "You are pathetic. You can't justify this bullshit, so please stop talking because you're making it worse."

"No, Mary. You need to listen. All of that was before we started over. I still want my family. I still want this marriage to work."

I stormed down to the living room, and when Charles followed I charged toward him like a bull, swinging my tiny fists with fury at his chest until they throbbed in pain. My emotions were running over. Tears were streaming down my face. I knew Charles wasn't taking my breakdown seriously because I'd supposedly reached my breaking point several times with him before, but there wouldn't be any mending of my heart today. Even if Jesus Christ Himself spoke into me and asked me to forgive him for getting another woman pregnant, the answer would still be "absolutely not." His side life had ruined my forever after.

"Naw, you don't love anybody but yourself. Oh, and maybe that bastard baby you've got brewing in that bitch's belly," I spat, hurting myself every time I said it. I wanted the baby I'd lost. My mouth was going a mile a minute. I was infuriated and needed to make sure Charles understood the magnitude of my anger. I had tolerated and sometimes even endorsed his cheating within our marriage by not leaving and forgiving him so many times, but this was the final straw.

Pushing me back off him, he held my arms and shook me like he was trying to shake some sense into me. "Mary, calm down."

I yanked away from him and grabbed the closest object to me. Throwing the remote into the fifty-inch television that was mounted to the wall, the power flicked off as the screen shattered. Pieces of glass flew all over the living room, specks even hitting Charles.

"Hey, don't throw shit else," he yelled, looking at the television in disbelief. "You ain't gonna be tearing up nothing I worked hard for to bring up in here."

"Fuck you and watch me."

First picture frames from our wedding went flying toward Charles's head. Then it was the laptop he'd been using to have cybersex with women. I threw it as hard as I could against the hardwood floor. I flew through the house like a madwoman, lashing out with a broken heart. However, before I could tear anything else up, Charles swooped me up like a flimsy ragdoll and body-slammed me down to the floor.

My yells turned to whimpers as I fought until my body was drained. My hair was mangled from tussling with Charles as he tried to restrain me, and my heart ached because even though he vowed to stop hurting me, he never did. I didn't know why, but simply refused to be faithful. I no longer felt like I was to blame or there was something wrong with me. I had been his wife, his queen, and the mother of his children for years, the only woman to have all of those titles until now.

"You'll never be nothing but a dog, Charles. I have let you have side pieces and whores our whole marriage without giving you a rough time. Why couldn't you just fucking put a condom on? Yeah, why? Answer that fucking million dollar question."

Overcome with emotion, rage, and hurt, I rushed into the kitchen and swiped the Williams-Sonoma butcher knife from the counter. Marching with the intent to fuck shit up, I was going to be a force to be reckoned with whether Charles wanted to accept it or not. I usually used this knife for cutting up vegetables for their dinner, but I was now about to slice and dice Charles if he didn't leave the house. The sight of his face made me sick.

"Put that knife down, Mary." Charles looked unworried that his wife was holding a sharp blade.

"Get out," I shouted, waving the knife in the air. Running toward him, I swung the blade toward his groin, but he caught my wrist in midair and twisted until I screamed and dropped the handle in pain.

"If you had cut me, I would have had to kill you. So do us both a favor and chill the fuck down." I was sure Charles didn't think our fussing and fighting would come to this. I was sure he was trying to think of a way to get me to simmer down, but my irrationality had already set in.

"Get out," I screamed even louder than the first time. I saw red, and not the in-love type of red I'd been blinded by for years.

"Let's just talk and get through this, baby. You've got every right to feel betrayed, but I don't want to leave my home." Charles's tone was sweet yet condescending.

"Get out! Get out! Get yo' ass out of our house, Charles. This was not your home when you were making a baby with that ho, so go." I started breaking almost every dish, pan, and glass in the drying rack. "Get out."

Charles jumped out the way just before a pot crashed against the kitchen table, making one large crack that spread across the tapered glass. From the terrified look on his face, he knew he had lost the battle and it was time to go.

Charles Bivens

I strategically ran through the house with Mary close on my heels. She'd told me to leave, flung dishes in my direction, and even tried stabbing me all in one night. Even though she had every right to be infuriated at me for the baby and all the shit I had put her through, she overreacted, and I was trying hard not to react on her.

"I am begging yo' crazy ass to please calm down," I shouted over my shoulder, headed straight toward our bedroom to pack. "You've gone too far."

"How can I calm down when you keep ruining our marriage? How dare you say I've gone too far when you are the one who's been cheating? Don't try to flip this all on me, Charles. I don't have to digest the bullshit you keep bringing to the table." Mary's feelings were all over the place.

Mary's rant was cut short by four heavy knocks at the door.

"Police, open up!"

We were still and quiet, never having had the cops called on us before and especially for domestic violence. I wanted this crap to go away so the news wouldn't spread like wildfire.

"Sir, ma'am, police. We're Officers Tinsley and Crowley. Open up," one of them commanded even louder.

We were both stopped in our tracks. Although we'd been screaming and arguing with one another, in addition to Mary tearing up everything her hands touched within the house, neither of us thought the police would be at our front door. Mary froze, silent because she knew she'd been the one to be the most destructive, while I stood mute not wanting to eventually become target practice.

They started knocking again, which sounded more like swift kicks.

"We know you're in there, of course. Please cooperate by opening up. Mr. and Mrs. Bivens?" The police were relentless.

Our neighbors had obviously called them in and given names. Up until this day, they'd never seen or heard us fight. But today, the mayhem going on within our home that was pouring out into the reserved suburban community wasn't tolerable.

"What should we do?" Mary's voice was quieter than a church mouse creeping on Easter Sunday.

"It ain't like we got much of a choice, Mary." I shook my head. "Had you taken a chill pill like I prescribed, their redneck asses wouldn't be at our door."

Wiping the sweat from his face and trying to fix his tattered appearance, he knew the cops were already standing with discrimination and a few assumptions about black men, so he didn't want to look to fit the part.

"Naw, motherfucka, if you knew how to keep that toddler dick of yours in yo' pants we wouldn't be in this situation," Mary hissed, and then darted to the door. Hearing Charles continuously blame her for him being blatantly wrong fueled her aggression while pushing down her fear of the law.

The officers went to knock again when Mary swung the door open. Their mouths dropped open, and their hot hands went for their weapons. Mary's hair was all over her head, her shirt was torn to the point of exposing her breasts, and all the makeup she'd applied was smeared across her usually beautiful face.

"Ma'am, is everything okay in there? We've gotten five calls of yelling and noises of assault coming from within your home. Are you Mrs. Mary Bivens?"

Mary was slightly thrown back at the officer knowing her full government-issued name. Taking a look past them, she noticed a few cocky neighbors standing in her yard with scowls and judgmental faces, even this early in the morning. She turned her face up then responded, "Yeah, that's me. And yes, everything in here is fine." She thought about going against the grain and having her husband locked up for the bruise around her wrist, but she knew that was the ultimate betrayal. Charles deserved to be divorced, not ripped of his freedom.

"Are you sure, ma'am? If something is wrong, we can help you." One of the officers tried to sound concerned.

"If I needed you guys, I would've called, no disrespect." Mary shifted her weight to the side. "My nosy-ass neighbors can't seem to respect the privacy me and my husband value. We were having a very important conversation that you're keeping me from. So if you don't mind—" Mary's words were abruptly cut off.

"Excuse me, sirs, I was actually done with the conversation and about to leave. I have my bags here." I appeared with my appearance totally transformed. When Mary went to answer the door then attempted to stall or get rid of the cops, I'd changed and thrown a few outfits into a duffel bag for the road. I feared and hated the cops, yet I wanted a way out.

They looked at me then looked at Mary with puzzled eyes. Being cops, they were accustomed to domestic disputes where both sides told two different stories. On any given day, they'd call in for the coroner because some bickering couple finally nailed their failing relationship. So far I'd been to be willing to vacate the premises without being strong-armed or detained, and I was sure this was not only a shock to them but a relief as well.

"What in the fuck?" Mary's words fell on deaf ears. She was outnumbered as the three of us men bonded. Color meant nothing; it was all about male testosterone.

"Of course, sir. I can take your statement as I walk you to your vehicle. My partner can stay here with your wife."

As Mary had, Charles took note of the officer knowing too much about him and her. *If I ever make it back home, I'ma pay these nosy cocksuckers back. And that's my word one hundred.* Charles was a hot boy outside of his suburban lifestyle. And having a badged white boy walking so close to him made the hair on his arms stand up. The pistol and weed that was only a few feet away in his bag lingered on his mind. *Let me get rid of this honky pig before I be in some scalding-hot shit.* Charles knew the mandatory jail sentence for being caught with an illegal firearm.

"All I wanna do is get in my car and hit the road. Me and my wife need a few days apart, sir. And that's exactly what I plan to give us both." The tone in my voice was strategic. When I saw the officer's tight posture and stern stance lighten up, I went in for the magical line that won over all two-legged creatures with penises. "You know how women can be."

"I have a wife at home, sir. I surely understand." He revealed his truth.

The officer and I shared a light laugh then suddenly became aware of the neighbors perched or up close with wide eyes and open ears. The officer quickly resumed his original rigid demeanor. I picked up on the imbalance of his behavior then thought quicker on my toes. Being a man living a double with different women, this was something I did often.

"You spoke of a report on the porch, Officer. What exactly do you need? I can give you my contact information." I was trying to come off as being cooperative.

The officer pulled out his notepad, wrote my cell number down, and then opened the car door so I could be on my way. If there is any reason whatsoever, we'll be in touch."

I didn't have to be told twice. I slid into my car, cranked the ignition, and then reversed out of the driveway of my home. You can't beat having your own.

Mary Bivens

I stood with tears in my eyes as I watched my husband of twenty years drive away. He didn't even look up to acknowledge me as he pulled out of the driveway. The brake lights never flashed on to signal he thought about coming back, either. I thought I might be hurt beyond repair. Our vows of "'til death do we part" didn't include an addendum of "unless there's a side chick."

Since the pandemonium was over, I saw the nosy neighbors were now moving along back to their houses, shaking their heads while mumbling to one another about property values possibly decreasing because of the "nigger-acting black family." I knew they wouldn't say the shit to my face if I confronted them, so I blew it off. I had gone to battle enough for one day.

"Ma'am, since your husband is gone, we can either leave or take a statement. He's given us his contact information in case there's a reason to bring him in for charges you feel are necessary to file."

I took one look at the beady-eyed cop and decided I hated all men. "Get the fuck off my porch and property. I don't have anything to say to your kind," I shouted as loudly as I could; then I slammed the door even louder. I thought, *I am really about to sign up to play for the other team.*

THE END